OTHER BOOKS BY WILLIAM POST

The Mystery of Table Mountain
The Miracle
A Call to Duty
Gold Fever
The Blue Ridge
A Doctor by War
Inner Circles
The Tides of War
The First Crossing of America
The Evolution of Nora
Darlene
The Gray Fox
Captain My Captain
Alaskan Paranormal
Some Boys from Texas
The Law and Alan Taylor
A New Eden
The Riflemen

Kelly Andrews
Sid Porter
Pure Love
Lost in the Ukraine
A Ghost Tribe
Lost in Indian Country
The Gathering of a Family
Wrong Place - Wrong Time
A Trip to California
A Promise to a Friend
A Stranger to Himself
A Change in Tradition
Hard Times
A Soldier and a Sailor

A TRIP TO CALIFORNIA

WILLIAM POST

authorHOUSE®

AuthorHouse™
1663 Liberty Drive
Bloomington, IN 47403
www.authorhouse.com
Phone: 1 (800) 839-8640

Published by AuthorHouse 07/24/2017

ISBN: 978-1-5462-0154-0 (sc)
ISBN: 978-1-5462-0153-3 (e)

Print information available on the last page.

Any people depicted in stock imagery provided by Thinkstock are models, and such images are being used for illustrative purposes only. Certain stock imagery © Thinkstock.

This book is printed on acid-free paper.

CONTENTS

PREFACE

AFTER THE CIVIL War, cattle ranches in Texas were growing by leaps and bounds. During the war, cattle roamed free as most of the men were off to war for four or five years. The cattle multiplied like rabbits. Many were claimed and driven to market.

However, the cattle in Mexico were not claimed and many large herds roamed south of the boarder. The men of Mexico were occupied by a revolution, so many cattle were available.

A lawyer out of Virginia heard of this. He had a substantial amount of cash as he had sold his eastern holdings because of a divorce. He advertised in several Texas papers for wranglers to make a cattle drive from Chihuahua City, Mexico to Santa Fe, New Mexico. This brought sixteen Texas wranglers to Chihuahua. They were tough and experienced with cattle.

A young man from Texas had left a ranch near Marble Falls, Texas to get an education in California. As he crossed the plains of Texas, he had several experiences that took him from a boy to a man.

He ended up rescuing a Mexican woman and her two children. He then drove them to Chihuahua where the woman had a house. There he met an American gunsmith who recommended him to the lawyer from Virginia to be the foreman of the cattle drive. There are several romances and an evil woman who hassle the lawyer and the foreman throughout the story.

You can view the covers of other books by William Post by going to his website:

novelsbywilliampost.com

CHAPTER 1

On the Trail

MARVIN ELLIS HAD been working as a wrangler on a ranch near Marble Falls, Texas. His mother and father had passed, and his two older sisters had married and gone back East with their husbands. He lost track of them, so now, he was all alone.

Working on a ranch you have friends, but no one really cares about you, as they are only acquaintances. Marvin had been loved by his parents, and missed their affection. His mother and father were loving parents, and both often stopped what they were doing, and gave him a hug. He missed that. However, he was alone now, and at nineteen, a man is supposed to buck up and live his life.

He had finished high school a year back, and had a fair education. Had his father and mother lived, he would have probably gone to the college in Austin. However, he counted himself lucky to have a job, as the rancher, J. W. Randall, had hired him because he was friends with his father.

Thirty dollars a month and found, it was a living, but it was surely nothing he wanted to do the rest of my life. He saved nearly every cent he made so he could leave Texas and go someplace where he could get an education, and make something of himself.

Mr. Randall liked to talk to the hands. Once he talked about having a partner. He said, "A wrangler must have a partner. I remember on a cattle drive in '41, R. D. Poteet was my partner. He saved my life a couple of times, and I saved his once. A partner is as needed as a horse, particularly on a cattle drive."

He gave them lectures pretty often, as he like to do that. Marvin always listened thinking he would someday need the information Randall gave.

Some of the boys thought him a windbag, but Marvin saw great wisdom in a lot of it. Of course J. W. was just reliving a part of the life he loved. He was a cattleman, and that was his passion. No one enjoyed tending to cattle as much as J. W.

J. W. had a daughter named Patti. She watched when her father hired Marvin. She had seen him several times in town, when her father talked to Marvin's father. She thought Marvin was the most handsome boy she had ever seen. She fanaticized being his girlfriend, and now that he would be working on the ranch, she could see him everyday.

Marvin could tell Patti idolized him. Just seeing her face, as she looked at him let him know she had a crush on him. As she was only nine years old, and he was nineteen, he saw no harm in stringing her a long some. He would smile at her, and tell her how pretty she was.

The other wranglers thought this was funny. They ragged Marvin about his nine year old girl friend. Marvin said,

"Hey, with this face, she's the only chance I have," and they all laughed.

On weekends he would take her riding, and even fished with her in the pond behind the house.

Mrs. Randall, Mildred, was using him to move some things out of the attic and said, "Marvin, Patti is really hung up on you. I've never seen a girl that young in love, but she's in love with you."

"I know, Mrs. Randall, but all little girls have fantasies. When she gets a few years older, she'll see that I'm just another cowboy, and move on."

"I guess you're right. I'll just let her enjoy being a little girl in love. I don't see how it can hurt. There are no children her age to play with. I'm just glad you take time with her. You surely make her happy. I will warn you though, she told me she was going to marry you, so even though she's only nine, watch out.

"J. W. said that when a woman sets her cap for a man, he doesn't have much of a chance. That really made me laugh because when I saw J. W. the first time, I set my cap for him, and was never sorry.

"I thought I had lost J. W. when Chad was killed. He went a month without talking much. I was afraid he might take his own life, as he loved that boy so much. Then he hired you, and you really helped him. I think that is why Patti loves you so much. Chad took time with her like you do.

"I have to admit, I sometime pretend you are Chad. I loved him too much I think."

"No, Mrs. Randall, no one can love too much. I know Patti loves me, and part of that is because of Chad. I didn't know Chad that much, but I knew Patti missed him fiercely, so I thought I would try to fill in for Chad."

"I thank you for that, Marvin. Let's just let Patti's fantasy play out."

J. W., from time to time, brought the crew newspapers and magazines that he had read. Marvin was reading a magazine that told about California. They described the weather as the best in the world. Right at the last of the article, it said, "*A man can get educated for next to nothing.*" That really caught his eye. He started dreaming about going to California. He said nothing to the rest of the crew, who thought the cowboy's life was the best in the world.

However, when Marvin got a chance to talk to Mr. Randall alone, he told him about his dreams, and how he had saved nearly every penny he made to have that chance. Randall said, "I've noticed you never go to town like the rest of the boys. You're dad would be proud of you, Marvin, if you do it. He even talked to me one time about sending you to college. However, the fire that killed your pa and ma took all his savings, too, as he never used a bank.

"How do you plan to get to California, Marvin?"

"I thought I'd buy a horse from you, and just ride out. I can stop along the way and work, but eventually I'll get there."

"I'll give you a horse, Marvin, and help outfit you to get you on your way."

"I would really appreciate that Mr. Randall, but I would like to pay for the horse."

"Okay, Marvin, but I will give you a good price."

Marvin was just turning nineteen, and Mr. Randall

outfitted him with a splendid horse for only forty dollars. Marvin knew this was far too low a price, but Mr. Randall said, "I'd like to think your pa would have done the same for my boy, had he lived through the war."

Word then got out to the rest of the ranch that Marvin was leaving for California.

Patti caught him alone and said, "I can't stand it if you leave me, Marvin. Would you take me with you?"

She said it with tears running down her face. Marvin had not thought of how it would affect Patti. He said, "Patti if a man is ever going to make a man of himself, he must strike out on his own. I need to build something if I'm ever to have a family."

"You will come back, won't you, Marvin. I plan on marrying you. You're the only one I've ever wanted, and I want you badly."

Marvin took her in his arms and said, "I'll come back in ten years, I promise," then held her tight for a few seconds and kissed her on the cheek. Patti kissed him several times around his face. Marvin smiled and said, "Those were goodbye kisses. I wonder if in ten years you will have some hello kisses for me." Patti took this to mean that Marvin would come back and marry her.

"It will just be ten more years of me loving you, so I will probably love you more. I know you have to make something of yourself, so I will be proud of you."

All the crew wished him good luck, and he was off with everyone waving goodbye.

Just before Marvin left, Mr. Randall put a Winchester in

his rifle sleeve and a box of shells in his saddlebag. He said, "I'll sleep better knowing you're well armed."

Marvin smiled and said, Thanks, Mr. Randall."

Mrs. Randall looked at Patti when Marvin was nearly out of sight and said, "I'll bet you'll miss him the most, Patti."

She just smiled at her mother and said, "He promised he would be back in ten years, and I took it to mean, he would be back in ten years to marry me. So, I just have to wait. I turn ten tomorrow, so I will be twenty, just the right age to be married."

Mildred started to say something, but decided to let Patti keep that good feeling. She knew that ten years was a mighty long time, and people changed a lot.

Marvin had thoughts about riding to El Paso, and then on to California. He had a bedroll and saddlebags, with enough jerky to last a couple of days. He also had beans and some coffee. Mrs. Randall had given him an old coffee pot, an iron pot to cook in, a tin plate and cup, plus eating utensils.

He made good time, but took care that He didn't overwork his horse. He rested him at proper intervals and took it easy. He had ridden for three days now, camping out under the stars. He was lonesome at those times, thinking of the Randall's and crew. Then he thought of Patti and a smile came to his face.

The fourth day he rode onto three men driving a herd of cattle of about two hundred head. As he rode up, one of them yelled, "Would you like a job? We're a little thin on drovers. Three of our men left the other day, and we could surely use you."

He thought, "*I'm going west anyway, so why not help them*

out." So he said, "Why not," and fell in helping drive the cattle. When it became dusk they just kept on driving the cattle. A full moon was out, and it was easy to drive them.

He rode up to the man who hired him, and said, "Aren't we going to bed the cattle down for the night?"

"No, we have a deadline to make. Our boss told us to drive the herd twenty-four hours, take a six hour break, and then drive them some more."

"Where are we headed?" asked Marvin.

"A ranch across the Pecos River. A cattle buyer is meeting us there to take them up to the New Mexico Territory. They need cattle up there, badly."

"Marvin asked, "But when do we stop for chuck?"

"We eat as we drive. Don't you have some jerky?"

"Yes, but I would surely like some coffee."

"We all would. I'm paying you double wages because of the hardship."

Marvin thought, "*Well, what the heck, I can stand it if they can.*"

Just as the drover said, they stopped at daybreak for five hours and then started again. The third day near dusk, he knew his horse was going to flounder at this rate. He had just rode up to the boss, when all of a sudden, there were ten to fifteen riders that came up behind them riding hell bent, firing their six shooters at them. It then dawned on him that he was riding with cattle rustlers, and the men riding in were going to kill or hang them. He turned his horse and it raised its head and took a bullet meant for Marvin. His horse dropped, and he cleared the saddle before it hit. He knew he must hide or his life would be over in a few minutes. He found a badger hole not far from where his horse had fallen. The hole had some rocks around it, probably brought out by the badger. He burrowed his way into it and pulled the rocks in and around the hole. It closed the hole fairly well, but in daylight it would be obvious he was there.

Riders were going everywhere. Two of them pulled up near him and their boss said, "I counted four of them, but we only have three. The other one is on foot, and we need to scatter out and find him."

About that time two riders brought his old boss up to the man in charge and said, "Sam, this one is the only one alive. He's wounded, but he'll live long enough for us to hang him. We'll have to take him into town for that, as there are no trees large enough to do the hanging."

The one in charge asked the rustler, "Who's the missing rider? If you tell us, you might have a chance of living." Now his old boss knew better than that, so he said, "His name is Al Tillman. You can tell him right away, he has the reddest shock of hair you've ever seen. He's not much of a hand, so you ought to have him pretty soon."

Well, Marvin's hair was dark brown, and his boss didn't ever know his name. Marvin guessed his old boss thought he would give him a break, even though it was mighty slim. Everyone was still scouring the area for Marvin.

After an hour looking, the boss said, "We'll ride him down in the morning. A man can be seen for miles in any direction out here. He won't get away. Bunch up the cattle, and we'll have some coffee. I'm tired after that ride."

They left the area where Marvin was, and went to where one of the men had started a fire about a hundred yards from him. As Marvin laid there, he thought about a stream they had crossed about a half-mile back. It was not much, but it was flowing water about twelve feet wide. He knew these men would be able to track him down unless he could find someplace along that stream to hide. The place he was at now, would be obvious to them come morning.

He knew he couldn't survive without his saddle bags, bedroll and rifle. His horse lay only about fifty feet from where he was.

A couple of hours later he moved the rocks out from where he was, and went on his belly until he got to his horse. He took his saddlebags, bedroll and rifle, and crawled for about a hundred yards. He then turned north away from the stream for about a quarter of a mile.

His boots had always hurt his feet, so he had bought a pair of moccasins, and would pull them off as soon as he reached the bunkhouse. He knew his boots would leave tracks that a tenderfoot could follow. He was hoping they would think he was going north from the boot tracks he left. After a quarter of a mile, he sat down and exchanged his boots for the moccasins he had in his saddlebags. He then turned southeast toward the small creek they had crossed, and tried not to leave any tracks.

He reached the stream, crossed it, and then walked beside it for a couple of hours. He was so tired he could hardly walk. It became light, and he kept on walking. He could hear horses coming. He looked in the stream and saw a slab of rock protruding into the stream close to a steep bank. He wondered if he could get under that rock, and if there would be air enough to breath. He took all his gear with him, and went under the rock. To his surprise, there was a lot of space when his head emerged. He felt around, and could tell it was a cave of sorts. He pushed his gear into it, and crawled onto a dry spot. He didn't think of what animals or snakes could be in there, but he knew it was certain death on the outside.

He went to sleep immediately, and slept for several hours. It was cool in the cave. It had been blistering hot the day before. He decided to just stay there for a day or two. He had jerky, and there was water. He slept some more. When he woke he didn't know how long he'd slept. He just knew he was rested and still alive. He worried that someone might investigate that rock slab, but no one did.

He could tell night from day by the light in the water. He waited two days, but then his jerky ran out.

Meanwhile, the rancher whose cows had been stolen, had hanged his boss from a tree they found on the creek. They had given up on Marvin. One of them said, "There probably wasn't another rider. They probably had that spare horse just for an extra. There was no gear on it, and no cowboy rides anywhere without his gear."

The rancher said, "Yeah, that makes sense. That rustler was just telling me that to maybe get himself off the hook. Yeah, when you think about it, that horse was just an extra."

CHAPTER 2

Trying to Get Out of the Desert

MARVIN SHOT A rabbit, then made a fire right there and cooked him, as he was very hungry. He wanted to cover as much ground as he could, though. He walked mostly at night, as the moon was still bright, and he could see his way fairly well.

As the rustlers he hooked up with had been driving the cattle west, he knew the rancher looking for him was probably from the east, so he kept going west. He killed various small game as he went. He had no idea how far each day he traveled. He just knew each day was a bonus, and further away from a hangman's noose.

He had been without water for over a day now, and was beginning to think that he may die of thirst, but then he spotted a line of greenery. It was a river. He thought it was the Pecos. He didn't think he had ever seen something as beautiful as that river. It was actually just a stream at that point, but it gave him life again. He rested a day, before he went on.

The next day about dusk, he saw a campfire. He watched from about a hundred yards and saw no one but a woman and two children. They were traveling in a covered wagon pulled by two mules. Usually, a person traveling in a wagon had dogs to make them aware of strangers or animals that may come upon them, but no dogs barked.

After observing them for sometime he yelled, "Hello the fire. I'm peaceful and coming in. It was a Mexican woman of about thirty that met him. She spoke good English and said, "You are welcome, Senor. We are out of food, and need a man to hunt for us. My husband died a few weeks ago, and we're starving."

He thought, *"I surely hadn't counted on this."* He could see he had to go with them for awhile, until they could get someplace where someone could tend to them. He then might be able to buy a horse. Rabbits were plentiful, and he was able to kill several. He knew they had to have something besides rabbits, as rabbits have no fat, and a body must have fat.

The next day they saw a steer, and it had no brand, so he shot it. It was a large animal. The woman was on it immediately, and had it skinned in no time.

Marvin buried all the parts that they didn't use, as he surely didn't want some rancher accusing him of rustling. He had a fire going, and she put on a roast as soon as she could. She then began jerking the meat into small stripes and drying them. They worked all day doing that task. Firewood was very hard to find, other than dry sagebrush, but he was able to find many buffalo chips and they burned well.

While they traveled, there was very little conversation. Marvin slept away from the wagon. He had time to gather his thoughts away from them. They came to a small trading post, and he could see that there was no place for the woman and children. He talked to the owner. The owner said that he was thinking about leaving, as there was too little trade.

However, Marvin was able to buy the things they needed. It took most of the money he had, as they were out of everything. The children would need to be fed properly, and the mules would need corn as there was very little grass on the plains.

The boy was named Tyro and the girl Teresa. They were four and five years old. The woman was Juanita Torres. He told her to call him Marvin. She could not say it very well, so he practiced with her until she was able to say his name properly.

Marvin bought fifty pounds of corn for the mules, as they were skin and bones. They rested two days there. He was hoping someone would come by, and take the Torres family off my hands, but no such luck. He even asked the storeowner, but he said he didn't want them.

During the time they rested, the woman told him what had happened to them. Some men had come by, and took their food. Her husband tried to stop them, and they wounded him badly, but he drove them off. Later he died. The only thing they could do was to go on. They were heading for Chihuahua City where they had a house. Her husband had heard how good it was in Texas, and decided that they should go there. It was not what he thought, and the people treated them like they were foreigners, which they were. The trip back had been terrible. They had to eat their two dogs to survive.

When she talked of her husband, she described him as not much. Marvin could tell she thought little of him, and she especially thought the trip to Texas was foolish.

Marvin knew he was in for a long trip, but he could not leave them. He had bought more ammunition, and now only had sixty dollars left. Game became more plentiful, and they ate much better. The two days rest had done the mules good and they were now filling out again on the corn Marvin gave them. They were traveling about fifteen miles a day, now, and they found trails that had been used. Marvin didn't even know where Chihuahua City was, but Juanita said, "Just go west. We will come to a town sooner or later and get directions there."

Twice they had seen riders, but they paid them no mind. However, a week out from the trading post, a Texas Ranger came by, and told them to watch for renegade Indians or bandits. Marvin thought, *"What could I do if I see them. I can probably discourage them, but if they really want us, they'll kill us."*

They finally reached the Rio Grande River. Marvin walked up and down it looking for a place to ford. He found it downstream, and they crossed with no trouble. The mules were still in good shape, but they were nearly out of corn.

They could see smoke down the river and Marvin stopped to investigate it. It was a small village. They decided to travel there, as there was a trail to follow that wasn't bad. The villagers had many gardens irrigated from the Rio Grande.

As it was now into July, there were many vegetables becoming ripe.

They found an abandoned adobe casa in which to stay. So they decided to stay in it and rest up. Juanita cleaned it up pretty well. Marvin bargained for some beds and they were now off the floor.

The children had now formed an attachment to Marvin, as he played with them a lot. The priest came by and asked if they were married. Juanita said, "Si, we were married in Texas."

Marvin was astounded, but said nothing. After he had gone, Juanita said, "Those priests are very nosy. I felt it would be easier if he felt we were married. There will be much less hassle."

That night Juanita said, "You can sleep with me if you want." Then teasingly said, "We are married now."

It was tempting, but Marvin knew he would leave them, and just knew she would become pregnant, then he could never leave.

She had a happy disposition, and came to Marvin and said, "Since we are married, you will have to give me a hug just like you give the children. So Marvin did. They decided to rest a week before going on to Chihuahua City.

Marvin asked about the route, and was told it was very dry with very little grass for their mules. However, he was told that game was pretty good.

Each night Juanita would stay hugged to Marvin longer and longer. He could see she had desire for him, but he knew it would be deadly if he began sleeping with her.

After the week's rest, they stocked up with corn for the

mules, and vegetables and staples for them. Marvin also bargained for an extra water barrel that fit on the other side of the wagon. He checked his wallet and saw they were nearly out of money.

It was arid and hot. He rested the mules much more often, as he knew if he lost them they were dead. When they would find a small stream, it would have grass so they would stay there awhile.

Tyro began to call him papa and so did Teresa. He didn't mind, because he loved the children. They both loved to get in his lap and hug his neck. When they did this, Juanita would lean over and hug him, too.

The second day out, they saw dust that could be Indians. They stopped so they would raise no dust, and camped for the night. Marvin was in hopes that they hadn't seen the dust from their wagon. He had his Winchester, and stayed near the mules. He had staked them out on some rare grass.

About two in the morning the mules moved, and he looked at their ears that were perked. He rolled over, and had his Winchester ready. As the moon was somewhat bright he saw someone about to get in the wagon. He sighted and squeezed the trigger. The person fell back, and didn't move. Marvin immediately rolled two times away from the spot he was at, and as he did he saw the flames of two rifles hit the spot he had been. He immediately fired in the direction of the flames and someone yelled.

Marvin moved again and was now nearly underneath the mules. Just as he arrived he saw someone trying to unhitch the mules. He fired at him point blank. It caught the person under the chinm and the bullet went through his skull. It was quiet then. After a bit he heard a horse riding off.

Marvin sat still, not making any movement in case there were more, and they were waiting for him to move. He sat there for another hour, then he saw movement. It was toward the mules again. He waited behind a bush that gave him a clear view of the mules. He waited another ten minutes, then saw someone rise near the mules.

Marvin already had his rifle ready and squeezed off another shot. The man dropped, but before he hit the ground Marvin had moved. He was behind the mules this time. He slowly made his way over where he thought their horses were tethered. He knelt behind a Manzanita bush. Just as he thought, there was a man holding three horses. He squeezed off another round, and the man dropped. A horse reared, but they were tethered.

He made his way around to the mules again, and laid between them. They were both standing with their ears perked. Marvin stayed where he was until morning. When it was light enough to see, he saw that the men were Mexicans. Probably banditos. He wondered why killing those men didn't affect him. He had always felt he could never kill a man, but when they tried to kill him or his charge, he had no qualms about it. It was just something that needed doing, and he did it. He waited another hour then went to the wagon.

When Juanita saw him, she burst into tears and grabbed his neck. She was hysterical for awhile. Marvin then realized she was in love with him. The children were both hugging his legs and he put his arms around them, and hugged them all.

He stripped the bandits of their clothes, boots and weapons.

Each had a pistol in a scabbard, a rifle and a bandolier. One had a large silver belt buckle that Marvin put in his saddlebags. He then took out their shovel, and dug one deep grave. He put all of them in the same grave. They were all naked, as Juanita kept everything they had including their rings. He then filled in the grave and covered it with sand, rocks and bushes to make it look like the rest of the ground. He was elated to be mounted again. One of the horses was outstanding, and the others were very good, also. He would sell the three if he could. The one he rode had a very good saddle with silver all over it. It was an American saddle, Spanish saddles were much different, so he knew the horse he rode, had been stolen. He hoped his horse was owned by the rancher who was going to hang him.

Marvin then rode ahead to scout, and enjoyed traveling much more than when he was driving the wagon. They arrived in Chihuahua City a week later. He took Juanita to her home, and helped her unload. He said, "I need to check with the local authorities. Is the law here honest?"

Juanita said, "So-so. They don't steal from the people, but they still hassle the merchants."

Marvin went by the office of the local authorities, and told them what happened. The head man spoke English, and came out and looked at the horses. He said, "That's Juan Estrada's horse and saddle. We have been looking for him for several years. He has a bounty on his head of five thousand pesos. I will give you the reward money, and give you a bill of sale for all the horses. I must warn you though, he has several men who may still have allegiance to him."

"How will I know them?"

"You won't, but they will know you. Why are you in Chihuahua?"

"I brought a woman and her two children back from Texas. Estrada tried to swipe our mules, so I killed him and three of his men."

"The constable then whistled and said, "You must be a dangerous man. They will walk softly around you." Juan has a ranch south of town. His brother runs it, but it belongs to Juan."

"Not anymore. He's buried out in the desert where no one will find him or his three men."

"You are a pistolaro?"

"No, but I won't be pushed around. You might pass the word, that if anyone tries to shoot me, I will burn down Juan's ranch and all the out buildings."

"How will you do that if you are dead?"

"My men will do it," he answered.

"The man whistled and asked, "How many men do you have?"

"Enough, and no one knows them. Some are Indians, and can shoot the flaming arrows at night, so let it be known." Marvin was paid the five thousand pesos and handed the bills of sale for the horses.

He had taken Juanita to the house her husband had inherited from his grandfather. It was a nice house, and Juanita was already cleaning it, and the children were helping. She had taken the mules around to the barn, but had not unhitched them. Marvin found a feed store and bought six bales of hay and some more corn. He returned and parked the wagon near the backdoor, then took the mules to the barn where he had left the hay and corn. They had a windmill with a raised tank. It fed water to the house, barn and garden. Although the garden had not been planted, there were many volunteers from previous gardens, so there were many vegetables.

Juanita asked if he would stay until she could be employed. Marvin agreed. He sold the horses and saddles, and now had ten times the money than when he started. He had Estrada's saddle branded and the silver taken off, so that no one would know it had been Estrada's. He traded Estrada's horse for a very strong gelding. Marvin didn't want anyone to know he had killed Juan, but word got out anyway.

As Marvin was walking down a street one day he saw a gun shop. He stepped in and met the gunsmith, who happened to be an American. His name was John Ahern. John bought all the bandit's weapons. Marvin then bought a very nice colt 44. Marvin wanted that caliber because the ammunition would fit both his rifle and pistol. In his spare time he practiced using the pistol. He could see right away, he was no hand with a pistol.

Marvin went back to the gunsmith and said, "John, I'm no hand at all with a pistol. Do you know someone who could teach me?"

"I used to be quite handy with one, Marvin. I'll teach you what I know after work each day if you'll buy me a quart of rye whiskey."

Marvin said, "It's a deal." Marvin worked hard and slowly became better.

Ahern said, "The speed of a draw doesn't mean a thing unless you hit what you're aiming at. Aiming at a man who is trying to kill you is much different than shooting at a target. Has anyone ever shot at you?"

Marvin said, "I hope you will not think this is a brag, but I killed four men not long ago, but it was with a rifle."

"Oh, you're the one who killed Estrada and his men. How did you feel about that?" "I didn't feel anything more than if it were a wolf or a bear. They were trying to kill me and harm my charge, so I never gave it much thought."

The gunsmith said, "Killing sometimes affects people, terribly. I think you're a good man, but I see your point. If someone is trying to kill you, you just do what has to be done. I think you would do quite well if someone were to draw down on you. You have a smooth draw, although not particularly fast, you're quite accurate. Always try to be smooth, and above all, accurate. They worked together for over six weeks. During that time Marvin's speed with the draw increased. He had great reflexes which John said was essential in a gunfight.

John and Marvin spent a lot of time together as both liked one another. During that time Marvin told John how after a year or so of being a wrangler, he had come west, only to throw in, inadvertently, with some cattle thieves driving a herd. John was impressed. He never asked Marvin's age, but thought him to be in his mid-twenties or older. Marvin had a dark, thick beard and mustache that he kept trimmed to about a half inch. His face was tanned from being in the sun, and it made him look older.

Juanita always had dinner ready for him, and as he came and went, people thought they were married. Juanita helped this along, by telling a neighbor they were married in Texas after her first husband was killed.

The children always called Marvin papa, and the neighborhood children could see how they adored him, and thought he was their father. He went to mass with Juanita on Sunday, and the priest assumed that Marvin was her husband, and that he had been baptized.

Marvin came into the gun shop one day, where an America stood. Before John could introduce Marvin, the man said, "I'm Charlie Thompson. I'm down here to buy a lot of cattle, and head them up to the New Mexican Territory. John, here, told me you have brought up herds before from Texas. I need a man who knows cows, and can take a herd north to Santa Fe. Could I interest you in the job?"

"That depends. I don't come cheap. How many cattle are you talking about?"

"I hope to have two thousand."

"How many wranglers do you have?"

"He said, "I hope to have fifteen to twenty by the end of the week. I have advertised in several Texas papers, and several have come from Texas. Will fifteen to twenty be enough for you?"

Now Marvin had not even considered he would be the foreman, but now he realized that Thompson was hiring him for that job. He thought, *Why not. I can use what Mr. Randall taught me. I think I can handle it.*

Marvin then said, "I've never pushed that many cattle before, but I don't see why not. When can I meet the crew?"

"Tomorrow morning. Meet me south of town where all those corrals are. We'll be gathering there at sunrise. You can meet the crew there, and make your decision then. John Ahern told me you are the best."

Marvin shot a glance over to John with a raised eyebrow. John just winked at him.

Charlie then said, "I have also hired a cook and he's assembling a chuck wagon for the trip."

At dawn the next morning Marvin was at the corrals. The first man he met was a wiry man that looked to be forty or so. Thompson said, "Monty Gebb, here, will be your ramrod. He then introduced several other men. Nearly everyone was in their mid-twenties or older. All were from Texas.

Thompson then said, "Listen up! Marvin Ellis here, is going to be the foreman. He's driven cows from Texas to hell and back. I got the recommendation from an old time friend of mind. He may look young, but he's been through it. He killed Juan Estrada, who the law had sought for years to arrest So, you know he's a tough man. I'll be riding along with the herd, but he will be in charge."

Marvin then said, "In a drive like this, every man must have a partner. Someone he can rely on. Many men have been killed because no one was looking out for him. J. W. Randall told me about a drive where his pard, R. D. Poteet, saved his life twice. This ain't going to be a Sunday school party. There's some rough country between here and Santa Fe, and there will be people who want to take the herd from us. There's a chance a body won't return from this drive. So consider it now before you start. Now, find you a partner you can depend on." As the men were leaving Marvin said, "You never told me my wages."

Thompson said, "Six dollars a head that you deliver to Santa Fe."

Marvin was astounded, but just said, "Good enough."

Thompson then said, "I'm impressed. I see you know what you're doin'. I've found that men follow a man they believe in, and I think everyone of the crew was as impressed as I was. By the way, who will be your pard?"

Marvin said, "Why you, of course, I expect you to watch my back, and I will do the same for you."

"Thompson smiled and said, "I couldn't have a better pard, but you have a weak sister here. I have never been a wrangler, and spent most of my time in the cities. I'm a lawyer by trade, and have studied the cattle laws and ownership with care."

"That may be true, but you believe in me probably more than anyone on the drive, so I think I have the right partner."

That evening Marvin dropped by the gun shop and said, "John, what the hell did you tell Thompson. He thinks I'm Charlie Goodnight?"

John smiled and said, "I told him just what you told me, that you drove cows from Texas, and have the heart to get his herd through to Santa Fe."

"Yes, but I also told you I was with those thieves only about a week."

"Long enough, besides you were a wrangler on a ranch, and know your way around. Try it, I have a feeling you'll be good at it."

"I hope you're right. If it works out, I'll buy you a case of rye whiskey."

Marvin went home that night, and told Juanita that he was going on a cattle drive to Santa Fe, but would be back in three or four months. He added, "I promise."

Juanita put her arms around him and said, "As long as you

come home to me. She then kissed him on the mouth a long kiss. Marvin thought, *"I better watch myself or she'll have me hogtied and branded."*

They left the next morning.

CHAPTER 3

The Cattle Drive

MARVIN KNEW HE looked young, but he hadn't shaved for over six weeks. He trimmed his beard, and Juanita had cut his hair so that it was not below his collar. He looked much older than twenty, which he had just turned. He felt older, now, having gone through what he had on the trail the last three months. He felt he could handle himself in most anything that would come up.

The first morning, before the drive commenced, Marvin asked if any of the crew had ever scouted for the army or a wagon train. Two men said they had, and a third said he had scouted for a short cattle drive.

Marvin said, "You three will be our scouts. There are bandits and Indians ahead, and we need to know where they are, and when we might expect them. You will not participate in the drive, but you will stand your share at night watch. If you see any trouble or potential trouble, come hell bent toward the herd. I'll then give this whistle." He put his thumb and middle finger on each side of his tongue, and gave a shrill whistle that was extremely loud. Each man now knew the whistle.

"When you hear that whistle form a line on me. Tim, you stay with the remuda. Phil, you and Brodie drop back and help Tim. Indian's love to steal horses, so be on your toes. The rest of us will handle the trouble at hand.

"We will drive the cattle ten hours a day. We will rest them one hour at noon or when it looks good, everyday. That will be when we have our noon meal. At that time the scouts will come in, and I will assign three men to be out at least a quarter of a mile from our camp. We will want to keep as much meat on the animals as we can. I don't want to pull into Santa Fe with a bunch of skinny cattle. I want my pard, to get the best price we can get him. He put his trust in us, so let's do him a job.

"Mr. Thompson has asked that there be no gambling or drinking during the drive, so if you have bottles of whiskey or cards, throw them away. I will not tolerate any violation of these rules. I will simply pay you a daily wage to that date, and send you on your way. We may be in Indian country then, but it will make no difference, you will go anyway. So make that choice now.

"I've been told we may be able to pick up a few head as we go up the Rio Grande River. However, I don't know if that will be true, but we can hope so. Are there any questions?"

No one said anything, so Marvin said, "Roll 'em."

The first four days went real well. If there were Indians or bandits, they could see it was a big outfit and rode shy of them. Thompson had given Marvin a map, and they would cross the Rio Grande River somewhere southeast of El Paso, then proceed around El Paso. They would go north just east of the Franklin Mountains then go over a pass going west so they could catch the river again about twenty miles north of El Paso.

The first problem that Marvin encountered was with two men. One was keeping the others awake with his snoring. One of the men told the snorer about it, and he became hopping mad, and called the man a liar. Now in the West, that was a time for gunplay. Marvin stepped in and said, Harley, the man ain't lying to you. I've been wakened by your snorin'. There is no sense in taking this to a shooting, because if there is any shooting, I'll be doing it. So take your sleeping duds about fifty feet away at night, and all will be okay."

Harley was still mad, but he picked up his saddle and blankets and moved them away from the camp. About an hour later, Marvin slipped over to where Harley was. He said, "Harley, you handled yourself pretty good back there. I have great respect for you. Make friends with Pearson tomorrow. If you do, he will be a lifelong friend."

Harley looked up and said, "I know I was wrong, it was just the hardheadedness in me. I'll do what you say, boss. By the way, I was impressed about the way you handled that. I guess that's why you're the foreman."

Lon Timber was a big man and a bully. The youngest wrangler was Tim Morton, who handled the remuda. He saw that everyone was well mounted. He checked each horse after the day and especially looked at their shoes. He could re-shoe a horse while they were on the drive, and knew a lot about treating soreness that occurred from time to time.

Lon, however, seemed to like to pick on Tim and call him

28

names like "mother's boy" and such. Marvin could see trouble brewing, but Tim hadn't said anything to this point, but he did wear a pistol as did everyone.

Marvin caught Lon alone on night-hawk and said, "Lon, I have a bone to pick with you." Lon looked up and said, "What's that?"

I see you picking on Tim Morton, and calling him names around the campfire. Why is that?"

"He don't measure up, and shouldn't be on this drive."

"So how is that. He keeps the remuda very well, and does the job I assigned him. If you continue to badger him, I will have to let you go. I won't have discord, and you're causing that."

"So you're taking up for that baby are you?"

"No, I'm looking after the herd. You are causing trouble that may cause us to lose a good man. I know Tim can use his pistol, and he may call you out. Then where will you be. Either dead or injured. I simple won't have it. So, can I count on you to stop it before there's real trouble?"

Lon didn't say anything, he was mad. He just turned his horse, and rode away. The next morning at breakfast Lon wasn't there. Lester Holt said that he came in, got his bedroll, and moved out. He had wages coming, but he was too mad to collect them.

Marvin generally rode ahead of the herd, and the next day he spotted Lon's horse's tracks. When you're a cowpuncher, horse tracks are like a man's looks. Once you see them, you can generally distinguish them from others. These, however, were the only tracks around, so it was easy to tell it was Lon's horse.

Marvin didn't think anything about it until near dusk that day. He could see buzzards circling about a mile ahead. Phil Aster, one of the scouts, rode with Marvin and they rode up to where the buzzards were circling. There, tied to a tree, was Lon. He was nude, and had been burned alive. His genitals were removed as was his scalp. It was a ghastly sight.

Phil said, "Should I cut him down, Boss?"

"No, Phil, I want the boys to see him. It will be a good lesson. This is a good place to bunch the herd for the night. The boys will want to bury him."

Everyone saw Lon tied to that tree. They buried him that evening. Not much was said, but Marvin knew everyman had his own thoughts about what he had seen. He knew the twenty-third Psalm and quoted it, after they had laid him to rest. Everyone said, "Amen," after Marvin completed the Psalm.

Tim Morton came to Marvin and said, "He might have ribbed me some, but he was a good puncher, and I have no hard feeling toward him. I would like to write a letter to those who may have loved him. If you have an address, I would be pleased to do that duty."

Everyone on the drive had given Marvin an address of where to send their things if something happened to them. Marvin calculated how much Lon had coming, and gave Tim the address and the money. Everyone in the outfit had great respect for Tim after that.

Everyone was unusually quiet the next day. Marvin spoke at breakfast and said, "Lon has warned us that there are Indians in the area, so be alert. I don't anticipate trouble, but we need to be prepared for it. I think if we are attacked they will hit the head of the herd, and try to cut out a few head. So, if Indians are spotted, I want everyone except Tim, Phil and Brodie, to head for the front of the herd. Those three know what they are to do to protect the remuda. We will stop the herd there, and everyone else will form a line about five yards apart. Ground hitch your mounts, and do it thoroughly. Then rest your rifle on one knee. Have your canteen with you and wait."

Marvin was right. The next day about twenty Indians were spotted by Phil and he came toward the herd in a dead run. Marvin knew there was trouble, and figured it was Indians, so he whistled. He could see all the crew heading for the spot where he was. They bunched the herd, and formed the line as they were told to do. The Indians came in a dead run, but the men were ready. The Indians couldn't see the men on one knee and came right to them. When they were within a hundred yards the men opened up. Not one Indian made it to them. They killed everyone of them. It was a total slaughter.

They spent the rest of the afternoon burying them. Marvin overheard one of the men say, "That's the best trail boss in America. How did he know they would do that?"

The other man said, "He's been through it all, and at his age. I bet he's not over thirty-five."

However, Marvin had heard J. W. Randall talk about such a try on another herd. J. W. said, "If we had known they would hit the head of the herd, we could have lined up and stopped them. However, they ran off twenty head of our best stock."

That night Marvin thanked the Lord for J. W. and the tales of his experience. He decided that sometime later, he would write him and thank him for all the valuable information he passed on to him. As he laid there, he thought of Mr. Randall's ten year old daughter, Patti. She was in love with him, and everyone could see it. When they were alone one time Mr. Randall said, "You had better leave before Patti turns fifteen, she's already set her cap for you."

Marvin laughed and thought, *"I told her if she did well in school and always minded her parents, I would come back when she was twenty and marry her."*

He remember that they both laughed and Mr. Randall said, "She has been a model child and we never have to get on to her about studying. However, you had better watch what you promise. Sometimes promises have a way of coming back and biting you." They had both laughed, as they both thought it was just a childhood fantasy.

Marvin thought, *"In ten years she'll think I'm an old man. I hope she turns out to look like that good looking wife of J. Ws. Then his troubles will really start."*

Patti had been with Marvin every chance she got. She would always ask him to give her a hug, which he often did. She would always smile and say, "Don't forget your promise, Marvin," and he would say, "I haven't."

***

Thompson rode up to Marvin the next morning and said, "Pard, you just keep making me look good for hiring you. Of course John knew you were that good, but you looked quite young to have all that knowledge."

When they were about forty miles from Albuquerque, a

group of riders came toward them. The scout had returned and told Marvin there were several white men coming, but didn't look hostile. However, he blew his whistle, and everyone formed a line ahead of the herd. They stopped the herd and everyman was in position. Marvin rode ahead with Monty about a hundred yards ahead of the men, and stopped while they waited on the men to come to them.

The leader was a big man who looked to be in his forties. Marvin said, "What can we do for you?"

The man said, "I'm Stan Guthrie and you're traveling across my grass. I will ask you to pay me a dollars a head to continue on."

Marvin said, "Could you show me your deed, Mr. Guthrie?"

This made Guthrie angry and he said, "I don't need no goldarn deed. I've lived here for ten years and everyone knows this is my range."

"Not everyone, Mr. Guthrie. I don't, and until I see a deed I will continue to push my herd forward."

"Are you calling me a liar, whoever you are."

"I'm Marvin Ellis, and I am not calling you a liar, I am simply asking you to produce a deed."

"I don't have a deed, but I don't need one. If you plan to bring your herd on, then I'll stop you."

"Then you are a liar, Mr. Guthrie, because you are going to be dead if you try. If you kill any of my men, I will burn down your house and every building on your ranch."

This got Guthrie thinking. Could this man be telling him the truth. He then said, "You can't get near my ranch."

"I don't have to. I have Indians who can shoot flaming

arrows into the roofs of all your buildings in the middle of the night. You see Guthrie, we are not easily intimidated by a sorry lot like you have here. If you wish to draw on me now, I will tell you that I will kill you before you clear leather, so is a few dollars worth your death?"

Guthrie could see that Marvin may be able to do just what he said. He then wheeled about, and they rode off.

Monty looked at Marvin and said, "I thought we were dead meat, Boss. You really read the book to them. Do you think they will try anything?"

Probably not. He may harass us some, but nothing major. He probably thinks I'll burn down his ranch."

Monty said, "Well, if they kill you, I will promise you that the boys and I will burn every structure on his ranch."

They settled the herd near Albuquerque, and the cook drove his wagon into town for supplies. Marvin had decided to have Thompson and Monty go into town, but the rest would stay with the herd.

After they had re-supplied the chuck wagon, Thompson, Monty and the cook went into the saloon, mostly to hear about anything that might be detrimental to them, as they traveled to Santa Fe. The Guthrie crew was at the bar and one of the riders for Guthrie was telling about Marvin talking to Guthrie.

He said, "The trail boss of that herd must have been at least six-feet six. He is the meanest man I ever saw. He looked like pure poison. He never raised his voice, but he read the book to old Guthrie. Guthrie believed every word he said, and I did too. I've never seen such a meaner looking hombre. You could tell he could blow half of us away before we cleared leather. I was so scared that I damn near peed my pants. I think Guthrie felt the same way, so he turned tail."

"How many men did this man have with him?" his companion asked.

"They were all lined up with one knee on the ground. There were well over fifty of them if there was a man. If that foreman didn't clean us all out, those riflemen would. Guthrie did the prudent thing and ran. I had more respect for Guthrie then, as I saw how near death we all were."

"Thompson looked at Monty and said, "I thought he was well over six-six. He might have been seven feet."

The cowpuncher turned to Thompson and said, "He might have been. I bet he could whip ten of any of us."

They had finished their drinks and Monty looked at Thompson and said, "Let's leave this place, he might come here."

When they were outside, Thompson said, "He might not be six feet six, but he throws a shadow that far." They both laughed.

Monty said, "Please, Mr. Thompson, let me tell the story."

"Okay, Monty. You tell it, then I will tell it again. Everyone will want to hear it twice."

The trip to Santa Fe was the easiest leg of the trip. They had lost very few cattle and picked up more than they lost. Marvin was paid a little over twelve thousand dollars by Thompson. He said, What are you going to do with that money, Marvin?"

"I was told there was some mighty nice country north of here in the San Luis Valley. I might mosey on up there to see if I could buy some land for a spread."

Thompson said, "Mind if I go with you. We might become partners. I know the business end like you know the working end. I think we could form a nice company to the benefit of us both."

"I would like that. I'm going to deposit my money in the bank now."

Thompson said, "Me too."

They outfitted themselves and said "good-bye" to the crew. Monty and Tim came to them and said, "We heard you are going north to maybe buy a spread. You're going to need a ramrod and a man who can handle the remuda."

"Well, pack up and come with us," Thompson said.

"Pass the word to the others that if we buy, they have a job."

That evening, they decided to have a drink. They were at the bar maybe a half hour talking about their trip, when Guthrie and some of his men came into the Saloon. Guthrie never went anywhere without an entourage. He spotted Marvin immediately and started toward him. However, Tim had a beer in his hand, and bumped into him spilling beer all over Guthrie. Guthrie had just bought the outfit he was wearing, and was outraged. Tim said, "I'm sorry, how clumsy of me."

Guthrie said, "You ain't near as sorry as you're going to be, and took a vicious swing at Tim. However, Tim ducked the swing, while bending over retrieving Guthrie's new hat. Guthrie was now off balanced, and as he turned to swing again, Tim hooked his shoe on Guthrie's ankle, and Guthrie hit the floor.

Tim said, "My, I am clumsy tonight, and then stepped on

Guthrie's hat. Tim's shoe was dripping with wet cow manure, and spread it all over Guthrie's hat while looking like he was trying to pick Guthrie up.

Guthrie saw the manure Tim had spread on his hat and said, "Now, you've done it. I'm going to kill you with my bare hands."

Tim said, "If its a fight you want, I will accommodate you, but I must warn you, I know how to fight."

Guthrie was raging mad now, and took off his gun belt and coat. Tim changed into rubber soled shoes, the kind that laces up. He was also wearing a garb that most prize fighters wore in a prize fight.

What no one knew, was that Tim was raised by his dad who was a professional fighter. He trained Tim since he was ten years old. His father had retired from the ring just a year ago, and was living on the ranch he had owned for many years. The ranch was located southeast of El Paso along the Rio Grand River. Tim had read Thompson's ad in the paper about needing wranglers for a cattle drive from Chihuahua City to Santa Fe.

Tim thought this would be a great experience, and asked his father if he could go. His dad also thought it would be good for Tim, and told him to go. Tim was good with horses and had been taught by a Mexican cowboy about how to treat ailing horses. Tim had done this for their ranch for several years, so when he told Thompson his experience with treating horses, Thompson hired him to tend the remuda. There were around fifty horses in the remuda.

Tim had spotted Guthrie before they went into the bar. He knew he would likely come to the saloon. Seeing Marvin, he would probably want to fight him. Guthrie was well over six feet and weighed over two hundred and fifty pounds. Tim saw a pile of fresh manure and retrieve a small bucket, and filled it with the fresh manure.

Marvin was about to step in and stop the fight before he saw what Tim was wearing. He then knew that Tim could handle this by himself. Tim was nearly six feet tall and weighed about a hundred and eighty pounds. There wasn't an ounce of fat on him. He stayed with the horses at night, and each morning before dawn ran about five miles. He had done this the last three years, as he had thought about following his dad into the ring. However, his father had discouraged that.

The men in the room had taken the tables to the walls leaving a space for the men to fight. Tim stood in the middle of the floor. He had wound clothe around his hands so that his knuckles were covered. His father had taught him that. It would make a harder fist, and protect his knuckles at the same time.

Tim was dancing some as he waited, just warming up. After Guthrie had shed his holster and coat, he rolled up his sleeves a bit. He would enjoy bashing the kid until he could kick him to death, as he had another cowboy.

Guthrie charged at Tim swinging a huge fist. Tim deftly sidestepped him, and as he went by, swung a vicious right hand into Guthrie's lower back. Guthrie was stunned. His back hurt terribly. He caught his balance, and could see Tim grinning at him, which made him just that much angrier. However, he was much more cautious, now, and moved in on Tim flicking out his left, and waiting for an opening, so he could finish this kid off.

To his surprise, Tim came in with a stiff left jab, and then a right cross that buckled Guthrie's knees. Tim came in on him cutting Guthrie's face with each blow.

Guthrie then sprang at Tim trying to get his hands on him to take him to the floor, but Tim was too quick for him, and danced aside giving him another vicious blow to his kidneys. Before Guthrie could turn around Tim was on him planting blow after blow on him. Tim had him pinned against the piano so Guthrie couldn't fall, and pounded away at his ribs with devastating blows. Tim then caught him by the hair, lifted him up, and smashed him in the jaw. Guthrie fell to the floor, and didn't move. Tim was hardly breathing. He turned to Guthrie's men and said, "I warned him I could fight."

Everyone just stood there in awe. No one had anticipated the terrible beating that Tim had given Guthrie. However, as Marvin looked at him he saw a professional fighter. Marvin had once seen a professional fighter in action. He was fighting a local man twice his size. The professional just made the huge man look like a punching bag. A man beside Marvin at that fight had said, "Someone told me that the smaller man was a professional fighter. Those pros can anticipate every move and know, not only the defense for them, but what to do to counter them. I had my money on the pro even though the odds were three to one against him."

Marvin then saw Tim go back to a table. Under the table was a bucket of cow manure. He then knew that every move Tim made was calculated, from the beer spilling to the cow manure on Guthrie's hat. He turned to Thompson and said, "I never want Tim mad at me," and they both laughed.

Guthrie was taken to the doctor, and the word was, that he

would be in a doctor's care for a long time. Marvin thought, *"I bet Guthrie will even talk softly to his wife, now."*

They left the next morning. They had bought a buggy that carried their supplies, and the cook. Thompson said, "I think we should have as much comfort as we can. This may be an extended trip."

"Not too extended," Marvin said, and added, "The snow will be flying in a month or so, and I want to be back in Santa Fe by that time."

CHAPTER 4

Santa Fe

BEFORE THEY LEFT Santa Fe they had gone by the government land office. They were able to obtain maps of the area they were interested in. The maps showed the Spanish Land Grants, their dimensions and ownership along with a few homesteads. The entire area that did not have specific ownership was designated as open range.

Thompson asked, "How would we get title to open range land?"

The agent told them the government would sell them the land at three dollars an acre if they staked it or fenced it. He added that by fencing it, other cattle ranchers would know it had been bought. This sounded expensive, but prudent. What he didn't tell them, because he didn't know, was that ranchers who used the open range, would be very vindictive toward anyone who fenced property. The old ranchers figured they had prior rights to the use of the grass they used. They hated nesters or anyone who fenced property.

Looking at a map that had some mountainous terrain designated on them, they saw a Spanish Land Grant that sat in an area that was protected by large hills on three sides of it. They found the grant and rode through it. It had excellent year-round streams and good pastures.

Marvin said, "We would just have to fence one side, as the other three sides have natural barriers."

It was called the Cordova Land Grant, and had been given to a Spanish nobleman who had helped improve the mission in Santa Fe. The Cordova family had never occupied it. They were wealthy in their own right, and had holdings near and around Santa Fe. There holdings in Spain were considerable.

Not finding any structures, they thought it may just be held, and not used by the owner. They found many places where cattle could winter. They also found two areas that would be suitable for barns. There were also many acres that could be used to grow hay and winter feed. It was situated about fifty miles north of Santa Fe nestled in the foothills of the San Juan Mountain range. It was a valley with rolling hills and oceans of grass.

Monty said, "I think we've found a home, Mr. Thompson."

"I think you're right, Monty. I just hope we can find the owner, and make a deal."

They traveled back to Santa Fe, and again to the land office. The clerk said, "Why, yes. The Cordova family lives in that mansion just south of town.

The next evening, Thompson and Marvin went to the mansion. Senor Cordova received them graciously. Thompson had a gift of talking, and told Cordova that he was seeking a place to raise cattle.

He said, "I would like a ranch that would give work to many people. I want my employees to prosper as I prosper. I will build them homes, so they can live a happy life. The land on which I would like to build this ranch is owned by you. It is a grant given to your family many years ago, but has sat empty all these years.

Cordova smiled and said, "I thought I owed that property, but the Indians thought otherwise. I never tried to occupy it because of their hostility. I would like to sell the property to you, so people would have jobs. Do you think you could make it safe for them?"

"I can't guarantee their safety, but we'll do all in our power to make it so. Indian warriors are much fewer now that the war is over. There are many soldiers in the West who are prepared to keep it so. My partner and I are prepared to invest a lot of money developing a ranch there. We want to buy it from you. Are you willing to sell it to us?"

"I have no use for it, so I will give you a good price. It is about twenty thousand acres. Could you give me forty thousand dollars?"

We could, but it would leave us too little to develop the ranch. Could you find it in your heart to sell it to us for thirty thousand?"

Cordova smiled and said, "Yes, if you will promise to hire some Mexican people."

"Agreed, Senor Cordova, and you will be invited when our houses are built. It may be a few years, as we have to drive cattle from Chihuahua City, where cattle are cheap."

"I might be able to help you. I have a herd of English cattle that are ideal for meat. I bought them several years ago. They are on my ranch south of here, between here and a small town called Lamy. I think they will do well in high county, and they certainly produce a lot of beef per animal. They are worth more, because they are valued by the cattle buyers. They are called Herefords.

"I want to close down my ranching facilities. My sons have gone back to Spain to live, and my daughters' husbands are not interested in the cattle business. At my age, I do not want the hassle anymore."

"How many do you have, and what kind of a price do you want?" The price was reasonable, but the number wasn't. He only had five hundred head. However, they closed the deal, and Charlie bought them.

When they were out the door, Thompson said, "We're practically broke. We will need to put together another drive to build what we want. I will try to find a buyer for a thousand head. Are you willing to make another drive?"

"Whatever we have to do, I'll do it."

"Since I will be handling the business, I don't think I'm needed for the drive. You and Monty will do a fine job. You need to get your drovers together, and I'll need to find some cattle buyers."

They decided to keep the Herefords on Cordova's ranch north of the small town of Lamy.

When Cordova was explaining his ranch south of Santa Fe he had said, "It's too mountainous here in Santa Fe, so I wanted my ranch to be on flatter ground. That's why I chose the place north of Lamy. He also told them that he had heard talk of a railroad coming to Lamy. It would then be easy to ship cattle back East."

Marvin found most of the drovers had holed up in Santa Fe waiting to see what Marvin and Charlie were going to do. Marvin gave them the word that he would meet them in March at Chihuahua City. The drovers thought the wages were great, and agreed to meet him. They had talked among themselves, and knew Thompson and Ellis were going to buy a ranch, and they wanted permanent jobs working for them.

Thompson gave Marvin ten thousand dollars in cash. They had planned to buy two thousand head of cattle at five dollars a head, them sell half of them for twenty to twenty-five dollars a head in Santa Fe. They would keep half of the cattle for the ranch, and build the ranch with the money from the other half of the herd. Thompson thought breeding Herefords with the range cows would make for a meaty animal, that could stand the cold winters.

The trip to Chihuahua was without incident. When Marvin arrived the children and Juanita were happy to see him. Juanita knew that Marvin would never marry her, but she wanted to be with him forever. Over dinner the second night, Marvin said, "I have to make another cattle drive this spring. I have a partner now, and we are buying a ranch above Santa Re. It's a beautiful place."

"Please let us go with you, Marvin. I will come as your cook and cleaning lady. The children love you and they will be heartbroken unless you take us with you."

Marvin studied on this, while the children and Juanita looked at him anxiously. He finally said, "Okay." The children jumped from their chairs and kissed him. Juanita then got up and put her arms around him.

That night when the children were in bed Juanita said, "I know you love me, but not as a wife. I am too old for you, and you want a gringo wife."

Marvin said, "I don't want any wife, Juanita. I'm only twenty years old. I want to have a home and get established, before I take on such a responsibly."

"You have a home, here, Marvin. This is your home as much as it is mine."

"Thank you Juanita. I know you love me, and the children certainly do. It will take some time before I can get a house in Santa Fe. The children must be in school, and they couldn't be educated on the ranch. For awhile you will stay here, as the children can go to school here. It may be two or three years before I can accomplish the building of a ranch. After we move, you can rent your house. You can rent it real cheap to people who need a place to stay. I don't want you to sell this house, as it is a safety place. If anything happened to me or bad things happened in Santa Fe, you will always have a home here for you and the children. There are probably several people at the church who you can rent it to." Juanita thought this prudent and nodded.

She said, "When the time comes, I will talk to Father Lento, he's a wise man and will give me direction."

It took three months to buy enough cattle for the drive. It was the last of March before they had assembled two thousand head. The crew was anxious to move the cattle, and the drive was on.

They all knew what to expect this time on the drive. They had all partnered up. Some of the crew had left, but others took their place. Only Marvin had no partner. He spent his evenings visiting with all of them, individually. This brought the crew solidly behind him. Marvin was always ahead of the herd, at least a quarter of a mile or more. His lead scout,

Brodie, was a mile or two further out than he was, but Marvin wanted to be close to the scout in case of trouble.

They crossed the Rio Grand as they had before, and then crossed the Franklin Mountains at the same pass as before, then met the Rio Grand River.

It was now early April. They always had the river to water the herd. They went at a slow rate, and every time they found good pasture, they stopped to let the herd graze. They had a good remuda and Tim said, "Them are some good horses."

Each rider had three horses that they liked, and Tim knew what horse went with what rider, and always had them ready to ride. Tim could shoe the horses and watched them for soreness.

Monty said, "Marvin, that Tim is the best with horses I've every seen."

Marvin said, "He's not too bad with his fists either," and everyone laughed. Brodie said, "I bet Guthrie is still sore."

Phil said, "I bet he hasn't said a cross word to anyone since Tim gave him that lesson."

Al said, "He probably didn't learn much, but it don't matter. I bet he wouldn't fight a ten year old after Tim gave him his comeuppance."

Phil said, "I know one thing, none of us would ever offend, Tim, in anyway. However, Tim has such a good disposition that no one would have suspected he could fight like that."

Brodie had a guitar, and everyone liked to sing. It was a muted chorus, as Marvin warned them not to make a lot of noise. He was amazed how they could harmonize, and it was a nice thing to hear.

Everyone liked the drive, The cook was Don Edwards. He

was good at his job, too. Don had a bad leg from a fall from his horse. He was over forty, and still liked to be with a herd, so he took up cooking. He had worked in a restaurant under an excellent chef, and learning from that, made tasty meals. Some of the men had been on other drives, and told the rest that Edwards was the best.

When they reached the place where the Indians had attacked them, they were extra cautious. Phil, the outrider on that side, said, "I went further west than I generally go looking for sign, but saw none. I don't think there will be any trouble at all." The other scouts were out a mile or so, and found no sign either.

They moved a little slower than they had the previous drive, and the new spring grass had sprouted, so the cows were fed well. The trip was about five hundred miles, but it took them well over two months. They picked up a hundred head or more along the river, and they lost very few. There were always accidents where a cow was killed. Edwards made some fine meals out of them.

They reached the Lamy ranch the first part of June. They penned a thousand of them in the corrals that Cordova had there. Marvin left Al, Reno, Lester and Ponce to tend them. Marvin put Al in charge, and gave him money to buy feed if needed. There was open range near there where the cows could graze. These were the cows they would sell. They drove the rest north to the ranch, which was a little over fifty miles north of Santa Fe. The grass was really good there. When they arrived at the ranch, the men got busy putting in crops of hay and corn for winter feed.

Thompson had hired men to construct two large barns,

one of which was completed and the other under construction. The carpenters were two Mexicans and knew their stuff. The buildings were put in strategic areas, so the cattle could be fed out of them come winter. Thompson had also bought the ranchland south of Santa Fe that Cordova had. He did not have the money, but Cordova let him pay it off as he sold cattle. Cordova had only a section of land there, but it was a place where they could hold cattle, while waiting for shipment.

The first year the herd grew by nearly half. At the ranch north of Santa Fe, Thompson had built a large bunkhouse where each man had a little privacy. Edwards had a large cookhouse that included a dining room, that would seat about thirty men, a large kitchen and quarters for him. Once a week supplies were brought. Edwards took over that as soon as they arrived.

Marvin lived in the bunkhouse with the men. Thompson bought a house in Santa Fe. It was a large house, and he had a room for Marvin when he came to Santa Fe. He talked to Marvin about cross breeding the cattle from Chihuahua with the Herefords. Marvin thought it a great idea. It worked well, and the herd grew each year. They would bring the yearlings in each fall to Santa Fe, and sell them. They got top dollar for them as the cross breed was better than any cow in the area.

One night when he was in town Marvin told Thompson about Juanita and the children. How he had helped them, and could not leave them. Marvin said, "Juanita knows I will never marry her, and I have never bedded her. However, I feel responsible for her and the children. I promised I would bring them here when I got established. The children need to be schooled in an English speaking school, so they can be educated. The school in Chihuahua City is okay, but not the quality of the schools here in Santa Fe."

Thompson said, "Looks like you have a family, whether you like it or not. People may look down on you, but I look up to you. You are the finest man I have ever met, and what you have done is honorable. I'll advance you enough to buy a house, Marvin. I hope it is near my house.

"Since you have told me about your life, I will tell you about mine. I was a lawyer in Alexandria, Virginia. I was in the war, but only as a paper shuffler in Washington. I married a widow of a man who was killed in the war. I thought we had a good marriage. However, my job took me out of Washington quite often. While I was gone, my wife was sleeping with a neighbor's husband, and his wife caught them. I was shocked, but my wife told me she had been sleeping with him before her first husband went to war, and always would sleep with him.

"I was so disillusioned with life, I sold out and came west. I had enough capital to put together a herd. I didn't know much about it, but then my friend told me about you and the rest is history. I hope someday I can meet someone and marry again. I go to balls and socials around Santa Fe, but the women are either too young, or have something about them I don't like. Some of the young ones are obvious that they are interested in me, but I want a woman who is intelligent, and talks about the things I'm interested in. My wife, Adele, was like that. Other than her sleeping with that neighbor, I really thought her the perfect wife." Charlie went on about the many attributes she had, and Marvin could tell that Charlie was still in love with her.

Marvin said, "Well, you've kept me so busy, I haven't even looked around." My goal, when I left Texas, was to reach California, and get educated."

"What are you interested in, Marvin?"

"I want to read the law like you do."

"I think you should go back East, and go to a law school there, Marvin."

"No, I want to go to Los Angeles. I want to go through college, and then on to law school, if I still want to by that time."

"I'll tell you what, Marvin, I'll send you through college at the university in Los Angeles. If you leave now, you could get there by fall when the semester starts. Monty can run the ranch. I'll move Tim to Lamy to run that end of it. Don't worry about a thing. I feel we are equal partners. When you get to Los Angeles, have the bank there contact the bank of Santa Fe, and I will give them instructions about furnishing you money."

Marvin said, "I must move Juanita and the children here before I leave." He left the next morning.

While Marvin was gone to pick up Juanita ant the children, Thompson found a house near the school for Juanita and the children. After Marvin arrived in Chihuahua, Juanita rented her house to an elderly couple whose house had burned. She told them to pay the priest fifty pesos a month if they could.

They packed up their wagon, and Marvin drove it to Santa Fe. When they arrived, Thompson showed them their new home. It had indoor plumbing and Juanita was so overjoyed and surprised, that she hugged Charlie's neck. The children were glad, also. Juanita told the children they were to speak nothing but English, so they would be prepared for their schooling in Santa Fe.

While they were in line to enroll in their new school, Tyro asked, "Can Teresa and I use your name, Marvin? It will help us. After just a pause, Marvin said, "I would be honored." Both children jumped in his arms and kissed him.

As he walked away he thought, *I'm glad they want to use my name.*

A month later Marvin left for Albuquerque.

CHAPTER 5

The Trip to Los Angeles

THE TRIP TO Albuquerque was uneventful. Marvin had picked out a gray gelding that was a walker. He decided to wait until he arrived at Albuquerque to buy a pack horse or mule, and then outfit himself for the trip to California. The first thing he did when he arrived was to go to the land office, and pick up some maps that covered the route he would be taking.

He talked to a clerk about the trip. The clerk said, "I haven't been over the trail to California, but I have talked to several people who have. They say to use the northern route until you get to the Colorado River," and pointed out the route.

He continued by saying, "The Indians in that area are Hopi, and are friendly. The southern route takes you into Apache territory, and they are hostile. Some are on the reservation at Ft. Huachuca, but there are renegades who kill as many white people as possible. I will say, they sometimes go north to the route you will be taking, so keep your eyes peeled."

The route he had pointed out was east from Albuquerque to a community called Gallup, then to several communities in Arizona until he reached Flagstaff. He would then travel on to the Colorado River. The clerk had told him that the trail was good, and he would travel with only hills to cross. He said he had heard that the game was not too plentiful, but that a body could make out.

Marvin went to a store that rigged people for trips. He was talked into buying a tent. It was a small army tent that had iron grommets and eight inch iron pegs to hold the tent in windy weather. The Clerk said, "If the weather is clear, and you want to sleep looking at the stars, the tent's a good ground cloth."

He bought two small traps to catch rabbits or small game. He bought all the staples for a long trip, and twenty-five pounds of corn for his horses, incase they hit a stretch that had no grass. The clerk also showed him two, four feet square, canvas pieces. He said, "It's dry out there, but there are squalls that come through. If it rains, use that small shovel I sold you, and dig out a couple of holes that will hold about three gallons of water. Then put these canvas pieces in them, and it will hold the water so you can water your animals." The clerk told him to buy extra salt, incase Indians were encountered. He said the Indians craved salt, and it may pacify them instead of giving them something of value.

The clerk talked Marvin into a wire cage, that would fit over the pack horse that would hold all his staples and equipment. The clerk then put everything Marvin bought on a large scale, and the equipment came to just under a hundred pounds. The clerk said, "You won't want more than a hundred pounds on your pack horse."

The clerk added, "I'll have my man deliver all this to you at the livery stable tomorrow morning at first light."

Marvin then went to the livery stable and picked out a good horse. It was similar to his horse and the hostler said, "He's a good walker, like the horse you have. He has mustang blood in him, and is really good on the trail."

The next morning when Marvin was filling the wire cage on his packhorse with the various items, a man stood by with his horse watching him. Marvin looked up and said, "Good morning, are you traveling west?"

The man nodded and said, "I've never seen anyone travel with such a rig."

Marvin said, "I haven't either, but the clerk, who sold it to me, was pretty convincing. The wire cage was only two dollars and he promised me it would save me a lot of hassle."

"That's a pretty large drop cloth you're covering your rig with, how come so big?"

"It's also a pup tent like the soldiers used during the war. It can keep a body dry during a rainstorm."

The man just shook his head and said, "If you say so."

Marvin said, "I'm going to California via the northern route. I was told that this is the safest and most pleasant weather wise."

"You've got that right. The southern way is a good place to get an Apache haircut."

Marvin said, "I'm Marvin Ellis from Santa Fe of late."

"I'm Tate, from here in Albuquerque. I have a mother here who is still kicking. I'm going to the Colorado River where I have a daughter. She's married to a feller who has a ferry near a place called Needles."

"Is Tate your last or given name?"

"It's my only name. Makes it simple for folks." Marvin smiled.

Marvin could see Tate was a man in his late forties or early fifties, and would probably be good to travel with.

As they rode Tate said, "I figured you for a pilgrim, but I can see you ride well and know something about horses."

"I tended to horses some, but I learned most about horses from a seventeen year old. That guy could treat a horse for ailments, shoe a horse and tell you more about every horse than you want to know. He was raised doing it, and his dad did a fine job on him."

The first night out, a tremendous thunderstorm was approaching. There was a small stand of rocks with an overhang that the horses could be shielded by, but with no room for them. Marvin was busy pitching his tent. He made it some lower which widened it, because he anticipated Tate would be with him. Marvin drove each of the eight iron pins through the grommets, then pinned down the two ropes in front and back. It was beginning to sprinkle and Marvin was hard at digging a trench around the tent to take the runoff from the tent.

Meanwhile, Tate had used his and Marvin's ropes to make a temporary corral to hold the horses against the rock overhang. It would protect them, and they would not be able to run off if they were frightened by thunder. When Marvin had finished his work and had his bedroll inside, he took Tate's bedroll and saddle and saddlebags inside the tent. He then went to the rope corral and began digging two holes near the horses, while Tate just watched him. Tate asked, "What are you doing?"

"I'm making some horse troughs so the horses can be watered tomorrow morning before we take off." He then put down the canvas pieces in the holes. "While I'm doing this, why don't you throw some wood against the cliff to keep it dry for a fire tomorrow morning."

The wind came first, then the rain came. It began to hail, and the wind was horrific. They both went into the tent. After the hail, there was a torrential downpour. The wind was so strong it looked like the rain was raining horizontal. It rained for over an hour, then let up. An hour later it began to pour again.

Tate said, "I see you know something about camping."

Marvin said, "I learned most of it from a rancher I worked for. He would talk on and on about his experiences in the wilds. The other hands didn't listen much, but I drank in everything he said. It saved my life about two years ago. I had started out for California and lost my horse to some riders, and had to walk. I came upon a woman whose husband had died beating off some white bandits. He drove them off, but died from his wounds later. She had a good team of mules and two children, so I took up with them. They were going to Chihuahua City, so I saw it my duty to get them there. We had some more trouble with bandits, but it turned out to be a good thing. I was able to ward them off, and picked up four horses."

"How did you get the horses,? Tate asked. I killed four of them, and the other one took off. I was able to get title to them from the law in Chihuahua City, and also a large reward for the bandits."

Tate didn't say anything for awhile then asked, "Did you find out who the bandits were?"

"Juan Estrada and his gang, they told me. I got a five-thousand pesos reward."

"Do you know much about Juan Estrada?" Tate asked.

"No, I did hear he had a ranch near Chihuahua that his brother runs. They also said they had been after him for over ten years."

Tate said, "Yes, I've heard of him, too. He was a vicious man. He killed a man and his family in El Paso. The man had heard he was going to steal the man's horses, so he laid a trap for him. They apprehended Juan and put him in a prison near El Paso. I heard he was young and a nice looking man of about twenty. The prisoners sexually abused him while he was there. That made him so angry, that when they let him out of prison, he waited about two months, then caught the man at home and killed him, his wife and all four of their children. He then burned every structure on the ranch.

"Everyone was afraid of him, because they knew what he would do if anyone offended him. He raided and robbed everyone within a hundred miles of El Paso, and that included Chihuahua City. Even the law was afraid of him, because he then had a several men who rode with him. You didn't know him, but if you had not killed him he would have killed the woman and her daughter. He would have probably kept the boy as he uses young boys for his needs. Yes, you killed a bad man. I guess you are pretty good with a gun."

"I'm surely no expert, but I can hold my own. Mr. Randall

taught me how to listen and watch horses and mules. He says they are better than dogs. They can smell things a dog can't, and make very little noise, so an enemy feels safer. I just stayed near the mules on the ground and listened while looking at them. When I saw one of the bandits trying to untie the mules, I shot him then quickly moved away. I waited and saw some movement and shot. I knew I had hit another. I moved again, and they shot at where I had been. I fired at the flames of their rifles and killed another. I heard one of them riding off, but Mr. Randall had told me this was an old trick. A bandit will pretend to ride off, but his partner will be waiting for you. I waited over a half hour or maybe longer, then I saw someone climbing onto the wagon, and I shot him twice. He rolled off the wagon, then I put a bullet through his head. He was wearing a large silver belt buckle that I still have. I never wear it though, as it's too gaudy.

"I again heard someone ride off, but I waited until morning, then buried four of them. We stripped them as Juanita wanted all the clothing. I sold their rifles, handguns and saddles for a huge amount of money."

Tate mulled this over in his mind. *"If Marvin had killed Juan Estrada, and three of his men, he was a good man to be traveling with. He was surely not the pilgrim he first took him for."*

Tate was a woodsman, and pointed out different plants along the way that could be eaten. At times they stopped, so they could harvest some of the plants Tate saw. He would call them by name, and tell something about them. Marvin was all ears, as he loved to hear and learn. Tate pointed to a plant he called Mexican thistle. He said, "The roots of that plant can keep a man alive if there is nothing else."

When they camped that night Marvin used his shovel to dig up some of the roots from a Mexican thistle, and after peeling them, cut them up in a stew he was making. Tate added some herbs he had gathered, along with some wild onions. The stew was quite tasty.

They were about a day out of Gallup, when Tate told him a story about a woman, named Gloria Hernandez. He stayed with Gloria when he passed through Gallup. He had met the woman by accident, and an accident it was. He was riding along just out of Gallup, when his horse nearly stepped on a rattlesnake. His horse threw him into a huge thistle bush. He had broken his leg, and had thorns in him from head to foot. He finally managed to pull himself from the thorn bush, but could go no further.

A woman was traveling from a sick friend's home and saw a saddled horse with no rider standing about a hundred feet off the trail. She thought this strange, and drove her two wheeled buggy through the bushes to where the horse stood. She then saw Tate. He was unconscious. She spent nearly an hour picking as many thorns as she could from him, then managed to get him into her buggy, and take him to her house. She set his leg, and put a splint on it. She took all his clothes off, and she, her aunt and two daughter picked all the thorns from him. Some were deep, as when she put him on the seat of the buggy, it pushed the thorns deeper. It took hours to remove all the thorns. Tate never woke, and they were all glad, as it spared him a lot of pain. However, the thorns had some poison, and he developed chills and fever.

Gloria was able to get broth down him. He was delirious for two days, but finally became lucid.

Gloria was an extremely beautiful woman. When she was thirteen, her father was selling Juan Estrada some goods from his store, and Gloria just happened to walk in from the back of the store where they lived. Juan saw her, and immediately saw he could make money with her. He forced her father into selling her to him. Her father knew that Juan would take her anyway, so he was forced to sell her.

Juan owned a house in El Paso, and had a Mexican woman there to keep house and cook for her room and board. He told the woman to train Gloria to please a man as, he planned to use her to pleasure white businessmen for a good price. The woman knew Juan's viciousness, and worked with her. Gloria did not want to do the things the woman told her about, but the woman told her she was lucky, that Juan owed a pleasure house where his women serviced any man who walked in the doors with money. She told her about the many diseases that went with that, and that few women lived longer than three years there. This frightened Gloria, so she learned how to do the things the woman taught her.

When she was fourteen she had her first encounter with a businessman. The man could see she was a beauty, and offered Juan five hundred dollars for her. Juan thought this over. He thought it a good deal. He would let the man use her for awhile, then steal her, and take her to another town, and do the same thing there. However, the man was shrewd, and knew Juan would probably do this, so he took her to a neighboring town, where he did business sometimes. He bought a nice house to keep her in. Gloria was now happier, and she liked the man, although he was forty years older than her. He was gentle and treated her like a princess.

The businessman lived in El Paso, and when Juan could not find Gloria he became very angry. He wanted her back, as she made a good income for him. Juan went by the man's office and asked him about Gloria. The businessman said, "I sold her to a man from St. Louis for seven hundred and fifty dollars. Not a bad deal, I would say."

This really angered Juan, but he couldn't do anything about it, so he left it at that. When Gloria was eighteen, the businessman had a heart attack, and died in Gloria's bed. She didn't know what to do. She had made friends with a widow, who knew her circumstances. The widow said, "Try to sell the house for a low price, and take the money and leave."

With the help of the widow, she was able to do this. She got five hundred dollars for the house. She also had some money saved, and took the money the man had in his wallet, which was over three hundred dollars. Then late that night, she took the man to a hospital in El Paso and left him on the steps.

However, the man who bought Gloria's house knew Juan. He was bragging to Juan about a week later on how he had bought a house from the girl Juan used to own. Juan puzzled over this and asked, "What was her name?"

"Why, Gloria Hernandez. You remember her." Juan's mind was turning now, as he realized the businessman had tricked him. He now wanted Gloria, and vowed to get her back. However, she had disappeared. He had all his acquaintances looking for her. He offered a three hundred dollar reward, but no one had seen her.

Gloria had bought a buggy and a good horses from a rancher she knew. She asked him never to reveal that he sold her the buggy and horses, or Juan Estrada may come for them both. So, Gloria traveled to the New Mexico Territory. She wore a scarf, so no one could recognize her. She traveled past Las Cruces as she knew Juan probably had friends there. She drove on to Deming, camping out, well off the trail.

Gloria had an aunt in Gallup who she remember her mother talking about. She decided that Gallup was far enough away so Juan couldn't find her. She finally arrived in Gallup. Her aunt had a nice home on the edge of town. Her husband had died some months back, and she welcomed Gloria with open arms.

Gloria was shrewd. She knew she couldn't openly own a business. However, that is what she wanted to do. She had heard that a man, who owned the hardware store, was wanting to sell it. She had been in the store several times, and met a clerk, who helped her. They had visited some and he told her about his family.

She returned to the store, and covertly told him she had a business proposition to make to him, but he must tell no one. The man came to her house late one evening.

Gloria said, "I have heard your boss wants to sell his business."

The man, Tom Dixon, said, "Yes, and I don't know what I'll do. We have a baby due in three months. This couldn't come at a worse time for us."

Gloria said, "I want to buy that business, but it's frowned on if a woman owns a business. I want you to go to the land man, who is helping to sell the hardware store, and tell him you represent a person, who wants to buy the store, and make a deal with him. I will keep you on as the manager at more than your are making now. Will you do it?"

"The man smiled and said, "You're an angel, Miss Hernandez. I'll put the business in the name of G. Hernandez. Do you want to work in the store?"

Gloria said, "Yes. I will act like I am your clerk, while you run the business."

It took all her money plus a little over a thousand dollars she borrowed from her aunt, but she was able to buy the business. Gloria called her new manager, Mr. Dixon, and he acted as the manager. It was a good fit.

However, about the third month after Gloria had left El Paso, she found that she was pregnant by the businessman. She had bedded the man for over four years, and never got pregnant. It was a mystery. Her aunt and she wondered how they were going to handle this.

Her aunt said, "You can cover your pregnancy for about five or six months then you will have to leave. You can tell Mr. Dixon that you have to go to California to help a sister of yours who is ill. I will follow you in the carriage. When you get to the next stage station, tell the driver you are ill, and will have to continue your trip at a later time. I will pick you up, and bring you back at night. You can just stay at home for the next four or five months. I will fill in for you at the store.

"A month or so after you deliver the baby, I'll drive you to that stage station again and you can arrive on the stage here in Gallup with the child. We will tell people your sister had died, and you had to take her child."

However, it was not just one child, it was twins, but it

worked, and for the next five years everything went great. The hardware business was doing so good they had to hire two more people. She paid her aunt back in one year. They told every one that Dixon had promoted her to bookkeeper. She now ran the business without having to act as a clerk.

Men asked her out, but she never found anyone she liked. She decided to wait until the right person came along. She was now twenty-four, but she didn't worry. She knew eventually she would meet the right person, and if she didn't, she was happy living with her aunt and raising the twins.

Tate came every year. He stayed with them coming and going. He always brought treats for the children and her aunt, and a special gift for Gloria. They were great friends, but Tate knew he had no chance with her.

CHAPTER 6

Gallup

WHEN THEY ARRIVED, Tate introduced him as a friend. As Tate had told him a great deal about Gloria and her sister's children, Marvin decided to shave the morning they were to arrived. He was a handsome man. When introduced, he was quiet and looked deeply into her eyes. She was startled at the instant attraction she had to him. He brought to her memory, what she wanted in a man. She had never had any feelings for men other than pleasuring them when she was a girl, but when she looked into Marvin eyes, they just stood there looking until Marvin glanced away and saw the children.

He thought, *"She looked into my heart."* Marvin then became scared. He had never had a woman effect him like this. It was not her great beauty, it was something else that happened deep inside of him that brought the attraction.

Her aunt said, "These are Gloria's sister's children, Lydia and Lisa." They were both beautiful children that looked identical. They both favored Gloria."

Marvin had never seen a woman with her beauty. He

was somewhat upset with himself for staring into her eyes for so long. Tate didn't miss a thing. He could tell they were attracted to one another.

Gloria's aunt had always liked Tate. He was a bit rough, but she thought of him during the years. She knew he had eyes for Gloria, but that wasn't going anywhere. She wished he would look at someone who was available.

She then said, "I have some coffee on, and left for the kitchen." Both Gloria and Marvin were self-conscious. They did their best not to be obvious about looking at one another, but neither could keep their eyes off the other.

After Gloria's aunt brought the coffee, and they were sipping it, Tate said, "Do you ever worry about Juan Estrada anymore, Gloria?"

I think about him three or four times a day. I will never have peace of mind about him."

"I think you will, now. A couple of years ago, Marvin here, killed him near Chihuahua City. He didn't even know who he had killed until the law saw Juan's horse and saddle, and he showed them Juan's belt buckle. You remember that big silver belt buckle he wore?" Gloria nodded and Tate continued, "So, you can stop worrying about him. Your new boyfriend took care of him for you."

Gloria's aunt said, "For shame, Tate. You shouldn't say things like that, you have embarrassed them both."

"I might have, but it's true, I never saw two people in my life who looked upon each other as those two just did. They're in love, and just can't believe it, but it's true."

Marvin gave Tate a hard look and said, "You need to watch your mouth, Tate."

It was real quiet then, as no one said anything, and just sipped their coffee. It was Gloria who broke the silence and said, "Tell me how you killed Estrada, Mr. Ellis."

"He tried to take our mules and I had other thoughts about that."

"How many bandits were there?"

"Five, I think. I killed four and I could hear another riding away."

"You said, 'our mules,' was someone with you?"

"Yes, a woman and her two children. Indians had killed her husband, and I wandered up on them. I helped them get to Chihuahua City where she has a house."

"Are they still there?"

"No, I moved them to Santa Fe so the children could go to a good school."

"Is she your woman?"

"No, she is older than me by ten years or more. I do care for her, and I love the children, but she is just a sister to me."

"Maybe to you, but I bet she doesn't think of it that way."

Marvin looked down. He knew Juanita loved him and wanted him. He was silent then and Gloria could tell she had hit a nerve.

Gloria's aunt said, "I hope you will stay with us a few days. I would like to get to know both of you better. We need a man's company, and I know the children will like it," and both girls smiled.

Marvin said, "I had better check the horses."

"Gloria said, "I'll help you." Tate just sat there as he knew they wanted to be alone.

After they left, Gloria's aunt Thelma, said, "I know you had eyes for Gloria, but did you ever think of me?"

This really startled Tate. He was too shook up to answer, but he took a look at her and she had a nice figure. He just had never really looked at her. As Gloria was so beautiful, he never gave it any thought. As he looked at her he said, "Would you want an old man like me?"

She teased him and said, "What do you have?"

"So he said, "A strong desire to make love to a woman."

This startled her, as she wasn't prepared for direct talk."

"She turned red and said, "You have embarrassed me, Tate."

"Well, you asked, so I told you. What do you say?"

"There is no place to be alone, and we need to know each other more."

"Well, you told me what you wanted, and I told you what I wanted. Maybe we can take a ride in your surrey, and get to know each other better."

"That sounds okay, but let's wait until tomorrow. I have to start preparing supper."

"Tomorrow it is. That will give you time to think over our situation. I haven't been with a woman for some years now, so it might take me a time to get back into practice. You can help me though."

"I hope you will shave and cleanup. There is a pump in our water closet and a bathtub. I hope you'll take a bath."

Tate thought, *I hope it's worth all that,* then looked her over again.

Outside Marvin started unhitching the horses, and Gloria helped. Marvin saw she knew how to handle horses, and she led them to stalls in their barn. She fed them, and as Marvin was putting the saddles up, he turned and she was there.

She said nothing, and they just stood and looked at one another. She then said, "Do you feel it?"

Marvin said, "Yes, and I would have never believed it."

Gloria said, "Neither would I," and they kissed.

After the kiss, Marvin held her and she held him. Gloria said, "I've never been in love."

Marvin said, "Neither have I. But I'm finding out about it."

"Before we get too involved I want to tell you, those children inside are mine."

"I know. No children could look that beautiful unless you were their mother."

"I was sold to a businessman by Estrada. This man kept me for four or five years. I bedded him, but never loved him. I will say I liked his love making though, and bedded him willingly. He died, and Estrada heard about it. He tried to find me, but I came to Gallup, and have lived in fear for the past six years.

"Do you still want me after hearing that?"

"Of course I do. The past is the past. I've killed several men, but I'm not a killer. You had to bed men, but that doesn't make you a whore. I don't know the first thing about a woman, but I know I love you."

She held him close and cried some. "What will we do? You are going some place, and I must wait for you. I know nothing about you, but that you have killed men, but I want you and I will wait."

Marvin said, "We better get back, they will be thinking something they shouldn't."

When they arrived the table was set, and Thelma was serving supper. They ate, and after dinner Thelma played the piano. Her husband had bought it for their twentieth anniversary.

The men bedded down outside, as they preferred that to sleeping on the floor. After breakfast Tate said, "I know you two have a lot to say to one another. Thelma and I will drive to your store today and tell Dixon you won't be in."

On the way back from the store. Tate turned into a little used lane, and Thelma came close to him. Tate had taken a bath, shaved and put on fresh clothes. They kissed some and Tate said, "We really need to talk. If we are serious, then the four of us need to sit down and think this out. I have to go see my daughter, but I will be back. I know Marvin was headed for Los Angeles to get an education, but I would think that may be sidelined for awhile. He already has one family that he has to care for, I wonder if he'll be able to keep two families?"

"That's a tough one. What will they do with Gloria's business? And a bigger question is, what are we going to do?"

"It would be a lot easier if Marvin took them back with him to Santa Fe. Then I could stay with you. It would be a lot closer to go to see my daughter, and I would like her to meet you." He laughed and said, "She will drop her teeth when I bring you, I can't wait to see the look on her face," and they both laughed.

While they were gone, Marvin told Gloria his life story, not leaving out one detail. He even told about Juanita wanting him to bed her.

Marvin said, "Don't give me any credit. I wanted to, but

71

I didn't love her, and I could see her having my baby. Then I would be stuck for life."

"Well, you're stuck for life now, with a woman who has been bedded by many men. The last I liked. He was a gentle man. He must have been forty years older than me. However, he was a good lover, and I enjoyed him. He would only be there once or twice a week. He loved his wife, but they never made love. I gave him something that made his life happy. He gave me a start in life. She then told him the story of her selling the house and coming to Gallup, where she bought the hardware store."

She looked at him and said, "Do you think you can afford two women?"

"I'll have to. I'm a partner in two ranches that have over two thousand head of cattle. One ranch is fifty miles north of Santa Fe, and the other just fifteen miles south of Santa Fe. We use that ranch to stage the selling of cattle."

"You are rich, then?"

"In debt actually. My partner told me to go and get an education, but my plans have changed. I know we will wed, so I think we should talk that over with your girls. Do you think they will understand."

"They will understand having a father. Every girl wants a father. Mine was forced to sell me. I understood that. I know it broke his heart, but if he didn't sell me, Estrada would have killed him and taken me anyway. He did that to one family whose father had him put into prison. He killed his wife and children in front of him before he killed him."

When Tate and Thelma arrived, the four began to talk. It was decided that Thelma and Tate would stay and see that the store ran well. Tate would take her place at the store. Marvin, Gloria and her children would go to Santa Fe.

Gloria took her buggy, and Marvin scouted ahead. They stayed at small towns along the way, but didn't sleep together. They finally arrived in Santa Fe. It was a bit embarrassing, but Marvin always met things head on, He took Gloria to his house where Juania resided. He introduced Gloria to Juanita.

Marvin said, "Juanita, this is my fiancé, Gloria Hernandez. We will be married soon. I will try to find another house, but for now, I would like you to keep her and the children here. You both will have a lot to talk about. I need to go see Charlie Thompson."

And just like that, Gloria and her children were left with Juanita. Juanita was shocked, and knew that was the end of here aspirations of ever marrying Marvin. When they were settled in, Gloria sat with Juanita, and Gloria said, "Marvin talked about you a lot. He said he loved you, but the age difference was too much. He will always love you."

Juanita sighed and said, "Yes, I love him and always will. He would never bed me though, but I wanted him to. I knew sooner or later, he would meet someone his own age and fall in love. However, it's still a shock. I wanted him just like you want him, but it is not to be. I will try to love you and your children."

"Marvin told me he loved your children as if they were his own. I will try to love them the same way."

Juanita said, "Will we live together?"

"Probably for awhile, but after we marry, no."

"That is best, It would break my heart even greater to see

you love one another. I will clean your house and cook for you if you want."

"No, we will be of equal status. Marvin and I will treat you like a sister. I see how you love Marvin, and it saddens me. I wish all people could have the one they want."

Charlie Thompson was shocked when he saw Marvin, but with his quick wit said, "Man, it didn't take you anytime to get educated."

Thompson poured them some brandy and Marvin told him the story. He said, "I don't know what happened, but it hit me like a sledge hammer. I've never been in love, nor even thought about it. Once I looked in her eyes, I was instantly in love. Sex might have had something to do with it, but it wasn't the greatest factor. When she looked into my eyes she saw my soul. I knew instantly that I was in love. She said she felt the same. Neither of us had ever been in love, and really never thought about it until we met."

"That's the way love is. I loved my wife more than my own life. Even after I knew she didn't really love me, I kept trying to convince myself that she would come around. Then she told me she had slept with this guy before, and even while she was married to her first husband. She said she had continued to bed him while we were married, and would forever bed him. She said he was married and had five children. Most of which were born while he was bedding Adele. She also told me she had slept with several of my friends. I couldn't understand it, but I don't think anyone will ever understand her. After she told me about sleeping with my friends, I couldn't live with that, and she was tired of me anyway, and cast me off like an old shoe.

"I don't know if I will ever find someone I could love. I still love Adele. I just can't understand how she can sleep with several men and think nothing about it.

"When are you getting married?"

"As soon as we can figure out what to do?"

"Where is she now?"

"She's with Juanita. I thought it would be best to just come out with it all. Gloria said she would talk and make friends with her."

"I can see why you didn't spend much time there. You can bunk in your old room, while we figure this out."

CHAPTER 7

Return to Santa Fe

GLORIA AND MARVIN found a small house not far
from the school. It was only four rooms. To Marvin's
surprise, Gloria paid cash for the house, and they were set.
That's when Marvin found out she had money of her own.
They purchased a wedding license, and were married at
Thompson's large house.

Juanita was Gloria's maid of honor and Charlie stood up
for Marvin. They went to a new hotel downtown for their
honeymoon.

A week later Marvin went north to check on the ranch.
Everyone was surprised to see him. However, they were all
glad to see him. He brought out a quart of bandy, and told
all the hands to get their tin cups.

Monty said, "What's the occasion, Boss?"

"I got married while I was gone. I got to Gallup, and met
a girl that turned me on end."

Brodie said, "I bet you returned the favor," and everyone
laughed.

"When you see her Brodie, you will be in love, too," and everyone laughed again.

Phil said, "I haven't been to town in so long I was looking at a Hereford, yesterday," and everyone exploded in laughter.

Marvin looked at Monty and said, "I'm taking Phil back with me, we don't want any strange marriages taking place," and they all laughed.

Monty then started talking about the herd, and what was happening. All the boys got into the conversation as their whole life was cattle. Thompson had devised a way of paying them by them having shares in the ranches' profit. It was unique, but all the boys liked it as they saw themselves as part owners.

After Marvin was satisfied that everything on the ranch was going fine, he said, "Next spring, who wants to go back to Chihuahua and get another herd?" and they all cheered.

It was now getting into winter. Marvin stated he wanted another bunkhouse built, and to write him when it was completed. The Mexican carpenters were brought back. Marvin had thought about a plan that could backfire, but he wanted to try it.

When Marvin returned to Santa Fe he told Gloria about the fifteen men he had back there with no women. He said, "I would like to surprise them by bringing out fifteen women after the new bunkhouse is completed. The women will then have someplace to stay. I want them to party for a week."

"Where are you going to get fifteen women?"

"I'll advertise in the paper, and see what I come up with. I'll have an age restriction of between sixteen and forty. I will say no matrimony is promised, but it could be likely. It would be a week of paid vacation, and a week of partying."

Gloria helped compose the ad. To their surprise, twenty-two applied. They disqualified two of them because they found they were married, and another two because they were fourteen. However, Juniata said she wanted to go. So they picked fifteen, and in early March they got the word that the bunkhouse was finished, and beds were sent plus some musician.

Gloria stayed home to tend to her and Juanita's children. Two stage coaches and a surrey proceeded to the ranch. The men were completely overwhelmed. They were all very polite, when they met in the new bunkhouse. The new bunkhouse contained the new beds, and they pushed them against the wall.

Marvin said, "These are the rules. The men will treat the women like ladies, and if you want to be treated like a lady, girls, act like one. You will change partners every dance, so everyone can get to know one another. If two seem to hit it off, then you can be named a couple, and stay together the rest of the time. Everyone can have three drinks, but not beyond that. I know what liquor does to a man.

Brodie said, "He's married now, so we all know what four drinks can do to a man," and everyone laughed.

The dance came off fine the first night. The men took care of the cattle in the morning and the couples talked until ten each night."

To Marvin's surprise, Juanita and Monty hit it off and became a couple. As a matter of fact, after just the first night there were eight exclusive couples. Every once in awhile, a couple would wander off to be alone. It was a wonderful week.

Marvin said, "Do you want to do this again next fall, after we drive the yearlings to market?" They all yelled, "Yes!"

He then said, "If any couple desires, they can build their own cabin. We will marry them the day they finish it. Two couples said, "We will start on our cabin, now." Monty came to Santa Fe a couple of times to see Juanita. She was taken with Monty, and Monty with her. He met her kids and they loved him.

After the roundup, and the cattle were driven to market, another party was held. However, half of them, were married before the second party. The ranch began to look like a village.

A cattle drive was then planned. Just Monty and Marvin were to go first, as it would take a long time to round up two thousand head. Half the crew would stay to run the ranch, and seven of them would leave for Chihuahua a month later. Tim was put in charge of the drovers.

Brodie said, "Does anyone want to argue with Tim about being boss?" and everyone laughed.

In Chihuahua the search began to round up two thousand cattle. They rode south to the Rio Concho River, and found hundreds of unbranded cattle. They searched for ranches in the area, and none appeared. They went to the community of Jimenez, and found ten men who had worked with cattle. They took them south to round up the cattle. They bunched up fifteen hundred head, and started north.

Marvin had bought a wagon for chuck, and also bought ten Sharps repeating rifles and ammunition from John Ahern before he left Chihuahua. He instructed his new drovers on how to use them. Only one could speak English, but was able to convey what Marvin had to say to them. Most had used a rifle, but none had seen a lever action Sharps.

Marvin said, "Your pay will be these Sharps rifles, unless you want cash. None wanted cash, all wanted the Sharps.

Marvin showed them how to bunch the cattle, and get into a fighting position when they heard his whistle. They practiced this a few times, and all had it down. The fifth day a scout came rushing in and yelled, "Apaches." and Marvin blew his whistle.

The drovers bunched the cattle then fell into the line they had trained for. Just like the first drive, the Apaches hit them at the head of the herd, and the drovers were ready for them. There were seventeen Indians, and not one of them made it to the herd. The men were elated, until they found that two of them had been killed.

Marvin picked up the weapons the Apaches used. They were a new carbine used by the army. He now had more rifles than he started with, and they were just as good as the ones he had given his drovers. He told the drovers to give the rifles of the fallen men to their families.

They were in Chihuahua two days hence. After the cattle were penned, Marvin bought five hundred head that he paid six dollars a head. The men arrived from Santa Fe, and they branded every cow before they left. He hired seven of the Mexican drovers to make the drive to Santa Fe.

They followed the same trail as before crossing the Rio Grande below El Paso, and crossing over the Franklin Mountains twenty miles north, then met the Rio Grande. Three days past Las Cruses the front scout came riding back at full speed. He said, "About fifteen riders are ahead coming their way."

Marvin stopped the herd, and all the men took their positions behind him. It was hard to see Marvin's men, because there was a lot of brush.

The riders walked their horses up to Marvin and the leader said, "We're cutting a hundred of your cattle as you're on my grass."

Marvin said, "Now how are you going to do that?"

"By just taking them, of course."

Marvin said, "If you draw your gun I will shoot you dead. The leader pulled his gun and Marvin pulled his smoothly and shot him dead. Everyone was so surprised that they just sat there. Marvin then said, "Does anyone else have anything to say?"

That is when all of them went for their guns, but they were cut down before they cleared leather. Several were just wounded, and Marvin walked up to one of them and said, "Who are you working for."

"Howard Martin. He owns this range."

"No one owns this range, it's open range. Ride back and tell Mr. Martin if we lose one head, we will burn every structure on his ranch down. We will have bows and shoot flaming arrows for a month if we have to. Now, take all your men on their horses, including the dead, back to Martin's ranch, and give him my message. We've done this drill before."

When they were nearing Albuquerque, a man with a badge came riding up and said, "Who's the owner of this drive?"

"Charlie Thompson, why?"

"I'm the county sheriff, and he's under arrest for murder."

Well, he's a lawyer and is in Santa Fe."

"Well, you are all under arrest, then."

Marvin said, "You're wasting our time. You draw down on anyone here, and we'll plant you in an unmarked grave."

With that the sheriff turned abruptly around and left. When they were now well past Albuquerque, the same sheriff came with fifteen to twenty men. Every drover was in position when they arrived.

The sheriff said, "Now, what do you have to say. You are all under arrest."

"The first thing, is, you have no jurisdiction here, as you are out of your county, and if any of your men draw a gun, my men have instructions to blow you out of your saddle, and he pointed to his men who the posse had not seen. Now what do you say?"

Some of the sheriff's men had already turned around and were drifting away. Marvin said, "I see some of your men are losing interest. Now, get out of our way or try to use your guns." There was no hesitation, and the sheriff wheeled his horse around and left."

When they arrived at Lamy, they had picked up fifty head. Three of them had the Martin brand, so Marvin cut them out and brought them to the sheriff. He told the sheriff of Santa Fe about his trouble with Martin, and the sheriff trying to arrest them.

Sheriff Yates laughed and said, He's tried that before. I'll have the territorial governor write him a letter to tell him that if it happens again, he will be arrested and sent to prison."

A week later Marvin was walking down the street to the post office to get his mail. Charlie was with him because they planned to have a cup of coffee and discuss what cattle should go where.

Just before getting to the post office, a man dressed in black with a white shirt stepped into the street. He was wearing a tied down gun and said, "Which one of you is Charlie Thompson?"

Marvin said, "I am. You think you're tough, but if you pull that piece, I'll shoot you dead. I've killed seven men, and if you go for that gun, you're going to be the eighth."

"Martin told me you were a city lawyer."

"I am, but I've also killed many men, most of which are better than you, so go ahead and pull that piece. I want to rid the streets from trash like you."

The gunman was now not sure of himself. He repeated himself and said, "He told me you were a city lawyer."

Marvin said, "I am. Either make your play or get off the street."

The gunman went for his gun, but Marvin just pulled his gun smoothly and shot. He heard a bullet go by his chest as he had turned. He then saw the red plume come onto the gunmen's right shoulder, and he lost his gun and went to his knees.

Marvin walked up, and kicked his gun away. He said, "I could have killed you, but decided that I wanted to send your boss a message. Tell him if I ever have anymore trouble with him, I am coming out and hang him in front of his family. Then I'm going to burn down every structure on his property and run off all his stock. Can you deliver that message for me? By the way, if I were you, I would find another occupation. The next man may not be as nice as I am." While he was telling the gunman this Marvin was replacing his spent cartridge in his gun.

He then turned his back and they walked on to get some coffee.

Thompson said, "Did you know you have a mean streak in you, Marvin?"

"I've been told that."

CHAPTER 8

Unexpected Trouble

BOTH RANCHES GREW, and they bought a lot of land between Santa Fe and their ranch to expand their holdings. The railroad had come into Lamy. It was too mountainous to bring the railroad into Santa Fe. They now had larger holding pens, and shipped a lot of cattle back east. They also sold cattle to speculators, and were making a tremendous amount of money.

Both Charlie and Marvin were now investing with railroads and other businesses. Cordova was moving to Spain and sold Marvin and Gloria his mansion, and all of its furnishings.

They had an office in downtown Santa Fe, now. One day Charlie came into Marvin's office with a letter. Instead of reading it to Marvin, he just handed the letter to Marvin. It read:

Dear Charlie,

You may have no love for me, but I still have love for you. I know I did a lot of bad things that hurt you terribly. My lover of fourteen years has gotten religion and quit me. He is now a family man. I think I have gotten him out of my system.

I think I have matured enough, so I could make you a good wife, if you will have me. I have never stopped loving you, but my needs were just too much for me at the time. I have matured enough so I won't need other men's love, and will hold only unto you.

Please forgive me, and give me another chance.

Love, Adele

Marvin said, "Do you believe her?"

"I don't know. I do know I still love her. What can it hurt to give her a chance. If she means it. I could have the life I always wanted."

"I say give her a chance. If I were you, I would have a legal document drawn up that says she will never be entitled to any of your holdings, and that she must sign it, and have it notarized before a judge, before you'll remarry her. If she will do that, I don't see how you could be hurt."

"You always make good sense, Marvin, but I'm a fool when it comes to that woman."

"Then make the document say, she is not entitled to any of your holdings, unless your partner agrees for her to have them."

"That is why I like you so much as a partner, Marvin. You have more common sense than anyone I know."

Charlie drew up the document and both he and Marvin signed it before a judge and sent it to her.

Adele had very little holding now, and was nearly desperate. She surely didn't like signing the document, but decided she may be able to get around it in time. She signed the document before a judge, and had it notarized. She then sent it back to Charlie. After receiving the document, he sent her money to come to Santa Fe. However, he recorded the document with the proper authorities.

Marvin told Gloria about the history of the situation between Adele and Charlie.

Gloria said, "As Hamlet would say, 'I smell a rat'."

"I do too, Gloria, but if Charlie is ever to put this behind him, I think he had to give her one more chance. He loves her too much."

"Do you love me too much, Marvin?"

"Yes, I would send you a deed to everything I own."

"I know you would. I knew that the first day we met. I love you the same way."

Adele arrived and she was a beauty. She flew into Charlie's arms. Charlie introduced her to Marvin and Gloria. Charlie put her into his carriage, but as Charlie was putting her into the carriage she sneaked another glance at Marvin. Gloria just happened to see her, as she was being helped by Marvin into their carriage.

She didn't say anything about it to Marvin, but she thought to herself, *"That woman has a fire for men that can't be extinguished."*

About a week later, Gloria was in line at the post office to mail a package to Thelma and Tate. The man ahead of her said, "I hope you won't think me forward, Ma'am, but I am new in town, and am trying to open a business here. I want everyone to know me, I'm Glenn Truan."

Gloria was courteous and said, "I'm Mrs. Marvin Ellis. I'm pleased to meet you.

"May I ask what kind of business you're opening, Mr. Truan?"

"My brother and I have been Pinkerton detectives for ten years. One day my brother and I were talking, and decided we could do just what the Pinkerton's were doing, and not just work for wages. We found out that Santa Fe doesn't have a Pinkerton Agency here. So, we decided to open up a detective service for the citizens of Santa Fe."

"That sounds like a worthy endeavor. I will speak to my husband, and tell him about your service."

Truan smiled, and handed her his business card. She put the card in her purse. However, she forgot the whole incident. A couple of weeks later they were invited to a party that was at the mayor of Santa Fe's home. They were having a marvelous time.

Gloria had to use the bathroom. As she came out, her eyes always went to Marvin. He was standing close to Adele, while Charlie was telling one of his tales. She saw Adele run her hand down Marvin's arm, then smile at him."

Gloria thought, "*That woman is going after my husband.*"

Two weeks later, they were invited to a ball to celebrate the fourth of July. It was held in an auditorium that the City had just built for this kind of activity. Charlie had asked Gloria to dance, so Marvin asked Adele to dance. Gloria watched very closely and saw Adele dance very close to Marvin, and put her leg between his at the close of the dance.

That evening, when they were getting undressed for bed, Gloria said, "Did you feel Adele's leg between yours at the close of the dance when you danced with her?"

"Yes, I did. It could have been just a slip."

"I don't think so. I think she was coming onto you. Don't make it obvious, but start watching her closely. I think that woman wants you so she can blackmail you into voiding that agreement you signed with Charlie. If she can get you in a compromising position, she may try it. She knows that you and Charlie are the closest of friends."

"I have never doubted you on what you think. I think women have real insight when it comes to those things. Men are like me, we only think of cows and good pasture for them," which made Gloria smile. He added, "I will keep an eye out, and if I feel her come onto me, I will not say anything, but will let her know I do not approve of what she did."

Every party that they attended Adele somehow got Marvin alone. One time she ran her hand over his privates. Marvin backed away and said, "I'm not interested, Adele."

"She said, "Whatever do you mean."

"You know what I mean."

Charlie came up and said, "Isn't this a fine party?"

Adele said, "I am really enjoying it."

That night, he told Gloria what had happened, and what he and she said. He then said, "You were right, she wants me. However, I don't think she wants me so much, as she wants me to destroy that paper recorded at the courthouse."

Gloria said, "I don't know, if I were her, I would be trying for you."

Marvin laughed and said, "Well, she has been known to like men a lot. Maybe we should see what she is up to with other men."

Gloria laughed and said, "I don't know how we would do that." However, she then thought of Glenn Truan, who she had never mentioned to Marvin. The next day she went by the Truan Detective Agency. She asked, "Will you keep everything I tell you confidential?"

Glenn looked at her and said, "Our motto is "Utmost Integrity."

Gloria then told Glenn the entire story about Adele. It took sometime. As she finished, she said, "I want you to keep that woman under surveillance. I want to know if she is seeing other men. She made a pass at my husband, but was turned down."

Glenn said, "She must be a fool to think your husband would look at any other woman when he's married to the best looking woman in the New Mexican Territory."

Gloria said, "Thank you, Mr. Truan. How much is this going to cost me?"

"That service is expensive as it will take round the clock surveillance. We will have to charge you five dollars a day. How long do you want the surveillance to go on?"

Gloria reached in her purse and pulled out a hundred and fifty dollars, and said, "This should cover the first month."

Glenn said, "My gosh, this is the largest fee my brother and I have ever made. We'll do you a good job. If anything is going on with the Thompson woman, we'll find out. I'll give you a report each week in writing, but not send it to you. I'll just keep it in our safe until this job is over. Let's meet at the Jefferson Hotel's coffee room. I'll be sitting in the corner. There's a chair that sits near. It's rare that anyone is near that area. Just get your coffee, and I can give you a verbal report without anyone being the wiser."

Gloria said, "Thank you, Mr. Truan."

Adele had met a handsome man, Robert Hargrove, who was in the social life of Santa Fe. His wife had a debilitating sickness, and never attended the parties.

Glenn Truan was always invited to parties, now. He always stayed in the background observing people. If you asked someone about him, most would say he wasn't in attendance.

Gloria never looked Adele's way if Adele could see her, but Gloria had several moments to observe her. Adele liked Robert, and they danced several times together. Truan could see them talking. He was able to lip read some of their conversation. He read enough to know that they were to rendezvous at a hotel on the outskirts of Santa Fe.

Truan knew the hotel, and went there. He paid the manager five dollars to put them in a certain room. Truan and his brother rented the adjoining room. They put holes in the wall so they could observe the bed. They were able to make photographs of both entering the hotel, then they went to the room they had rented. They observed the tryst, but were unable to take a photo because of the poor lighting. Adele and Robert met there nearly every week.

Adele sent Robert secret notes. She would write a note, and leave it in a crack of a brick wall near her residence. Robert was observed picking up the notes. Before Robert picked up the note, Glenn would pick up the note, and take it to his office to photograph it. The notes were filled with graphic language about their union, which gave Adele a thrill.

A month had now passed. Truan gave Gloria a complete packet of his observations and the photographs. She read them carefully, and decided not to tell Marvin or Charlie. She had a plan.

She mailed one of the more explicit notes Glenn had photographed to Adele. Gloria had paid Truan for another week to observe the meeting between Adele and Robert at the hotel where they met. Truan was able to photograph them together outside the hotel arguing. She was livid, as she thought Robert was going to blackmail her. He finally convinced her that he had not sent the photo. They went inside the lobby to try and figure out who sent the photo. They could not come up with an answer. The next day Gloria sent her a picture of Robert and her at the entrance of the hotel.

Robert said, "It's over Adele. My reputation will be ruined if this gets out. I'm done." Adele cried, but Robert said, "Crying won't do any good. Your husband will kick you out if he finds out, and may try to kill me. We're done," and he walked away.

At the next social event, Robert walked away when Adele came anywhere near him. Charlie noticed that and said, "My, did you offend Robert. He acted angry with you."

Adele said, "I know I shouldn't have, but I told him I had noticed he was getting wrinkles. It was said in jest, but he took great offense to the remark."

"Well, I will go to him and make it up."

"No, Charles, it would do more harm than good. He will get over it in time."

Adele thought and thought, *"Who could have taken the notes? And for that matter, who had taken the photograph?"*

After some thought she said out loud, "Gloria! She must have seen me come on to Marvin. I think she is following me."

However, after she thought about it for awhile, she thought, *"No, she has children to mind and wouldn't have time for that."* She knew that Marvin would never follow her, as he had little to no interest in her.

One day she just happened to read the sign over Truan's detective agency. It then dawned on her that Gloria could have hired the agency to spy on her. She read Glenn Truan's name on the door.

Adele then devised a plan. She wrote a note to Gloria that said, "I need to see you. Meet me in the park at one o'clock today," and signed it, Glenn. She knew if Gloria had nothing to do with this, that she would not know who Glenn was, and would ignore it. However, Gloria went to the park. No one was there of course, and she went home wondering what Truan had to say.

Adele now knew who was behind this. She then began to plot a way to silence her. She began to form an insidious plan. She told Charlie she needed to go to Albuquerque to meet her sister and that she would probably be gone a week. Actually, she had sent money to her sister, and told her it was impetrative that she meet her in Albuquerque on a certain date. Her sister, who lived in Topeka, Kansas, took the train. Adele met her and said, "You must stay a week. I have something that I have to do, and will be back in a day or two."

Adele paid a Mexican in Albuquerque to drive her to Santa Fe and back. She said, "I must come back the same night that we reach Santa Fe."

However, Glenn Truan happened to observe Adele taking the stage to Albuquerque. He told his brother that he had a moral obligation to see what Adele was up to. He rode a horse, and followed the stage. When Adele arrived in Albuquerque, he followed her to the hotel. He waited in the lobby, where he could see her comings and goings. He saw her meet a Mexican man. He followed the man to a livery stable, and asked him if he would drive him to El Paso.

The Mexican said, "I can't for a couple of days as I am taking someone to Santa Fe. I will be back tomorrow late, and can take you the next day. Truan now knew Adele was setting up an alibi. He followed their buggy at some distance, and saw them draw up to Marvin's house. Turan knew Marvin was in Chihuahua City getting ready for another cattle drive. He rode up to the house just as he heard a gun go off. He then knew that Adele had probably shot Gloria. Just as Adele was coming to the front door, Glenn rushed in and knocked her down. She lost the gun, but Glenn had her.

Lamps then were being lit. The Mexican, who drove Adele, took off knowing he may be implicated in a shooting. Dragging Adele with him, he went into Glories bedroom. She was dead. Shot through the head.

Neighbor's lights were lit and a neighbor came over, and saw what had happened. Marvin had no idea for over a month, what had happened. Adele was taken to jail. A trial was set for her. Glenn had all the evidence that was needed.

Charlie was overwhelmed. He went to see Adele in her jail cell. He asked "Why did you do such a thing, Adele?"

"She deserved killing. She was messing with my life. You meant nothing to me, Charlie, just a meal ticket until I could get enough money to get on with my life. Now get out of here, you're making me sick."

Charlie finally realized what Adele really was. He had wasted half a lifetime on a woman who was completely evil.

Glenn and the prosecuting attorney were able to keep Robert's name out of the trial. Although the prosecuting attorney talked to him, he told him he would do his best to keep him out of it. That cured Robert from ever straying again.

The cemetery was full with all who knew Gloria. Juanita took Gloria's two children. Two weeks later Adele was sentenced to life in prison, she was sent to a newly opened woman's prison near Jefferson, Missouri.

Charlie knew Marvin didn't know about Gloria, so he took Monty with him, and they rode to intercept Marvin. They met the herd south of Albuquerque. Marvin could see them from afar, and knew they were bringing bad news. He wore a grim face when Charlie rode up.

"What happened, Charlie?"

Charlie said, "Gloria was murdered by Adele. They caught her, and she has already been sentenced to life in prison. Had she been a man, they would have hung her. However, life in prison may be worse for her."

Marvin was stunned. He never thought about Gloria being in danger. Now the love of his life was gone. He said, "I could never love anyone the way I loved Gloria. God must have wanted her, badly. I don't blame Him. I would take her home, too."

Charlie said, "Monty will take the herd, Marvin."

"No Charlie, the work will do me good. I need something to keep my mind occupied. I now realized why I worked so hard to be successful. It was all for Gloria and the girls."

Charlie said, "It's all my fault, I should have never brought that evil woman out here. She ruined my life and yours."

"Don't blame yourself, Charlie. I would have done the same as you, if I loved her like you did. That's what I like most about you, Charlie. You're the most faithful guy in the world. I will love you forever. No, you did nothing wrong, it was all that evil woman."

CHAPTER 9

A Return to his Roots

MARVIN STAYED IN Santa Fe for another year. He mainly just went through the day without purpose. One day he came into Charlie's office and said, "Charlie, I'm going back to Marble Falls to see Mr. Randall and his family."

It had been nearly ten years since he left Marble Falls. He had never written the Randall family. He decided he needed to get away, and he wanted to tell Mr. Randall what had happen to him.

***

Patti Randall was about to turn twenty, and she had never entertained boy or man. She told her parents, "Marvin told me that he would be back in ten years for me, and he meant it, so I'm waiting."

Her parents both told her year after year, that she was living a fantasy. Marvin had just said that in jest. No one would tell a ten year old girl that he would be back for her in ten years, and mean it. It was just something he said to placate her.

However, Patti was adamant. She said, "Marvin doesn't lie. He was sincere with me. I love him. I have always loved him, and will to the day I die."

Mr. Randall looked at his wife, and she just shook her head.

The day that Patti turned twenty, she dressed to her up most. She bathed, and had her mother set her hair. Around noon, she brushed it out. She looked beautiful. Her mother and father just knew she would be devastated at the end of a day. However, at the end of the day, they were all sitting on the porch drinking some lemonade. They could see a rider walking his horse towards the house.

Patti said, "See, I knew he would come."

Her parents still didn't believe her, until Marvin walked his horse up to the porch. Patti said, "I told my folks you would come on my twentieth birthday, and here you are."

Marvin then remembered what he had told Patti, and just went along with it, by saying, "An Ellis always keeps his word."

Both of Patti's parents were completely overwhelmed. Mr. Randall said, "Get down off that horse and have some lemonade, Marvin."

Marvin dismounted and Patti came into his arms and kissed him a passionate kiss, then walked him onto the porch.

Mr. Randall said, "You must have one hell of a story to tell, Marvin. So let's hear it."

Marvin started with the time he left the ranch to where Gloria had been murdered. He tried to not leave out any detail. He ended by saying, "My roots are here with you, Mr. Randall, the prodigal son has come home."

Mr. Randall's eyes were moist and he said, "I will kill the fatted calf, I will give you my finest suit, and I want you to have the ring on my finger, Marvin. No one besides Patti could love you more."

"Tears began to boil out of Marvin's eyes, and he couldn't stop them. All that was pent up, and had never came out, was now flowing, and he couldn't stop them. Patti and he were sitting on the porch swing. She put her arms around him and said, "Just cry it all out, Marvin. I can see how much you loved her. I can't replace her, but you can love two people. I love both my mom and dad something fierce, but just because I love dad doesn't mean I don't love mom. You loved her dearly, but you can love me, too."

Marvin could not say a word, he just clung onto Patti. Mrs. Randall said, "I must start supper. It will be awhile, but later you will all be hungry. I never dreamed you would come today. Patti never doubted it. She has not seen one boy or man since you left. She said you would come today. J. W. and I told her many times that it was just a fantasy, but she has been adamant. God must know what he's doing. Praise the Lord you have come home, Marvin."

The next day, both her parents knew the two had much to talk about, so they suggest that Patti show Marvin all the new improvements of the ranch.

Pattie said, "Three of the old hands, who worked with you, are still here."

When they arrived at the area where the crew was working, they all were glad to see him. Jud said, "The only reason you come back was to marry the boss's daughter so you could rag us, isn't Marvin?"

Marvin just smiled. He had very little to say. They finally came to a giant oak tree on a ridge. There was a flat rock to sit on. He and Patti had sat on that rock ten years ago, when he said he would come back.

Marvin said, "I don't know if I can marry you Patti. I still have this deep love for Gloria. He then told her how they met, and how they loved one another."

Pattie said, "I'm glad you had her love, Marvin, but I have known since I was ten years old that we would marry. You won't have to compare us, as we are both different in many ways except one, and that one is, that both of us love you to your very soul. I will make you happy, Marvin. I will take that horrible feeling you harbor, and destroy it. You can't fathom the love I will give you."

"I think I can, Patti. Since I promised you, I will marry you. It may be awhile before I am totally yours, but I would bet my saddle, you will get me there.

"Patti, I'm a wealthy man now, and I want to take you on an extended vacation. I want to take you to New York, London and Paris. I want to give you things you never had. It is a reward for you waiting for me."

"That evening Patti told her mother at the dinner table, "In ten days Marvin and I will be married. You can write everyone to come. I can make everyone eat crow that doubted me. I know how everyone made fun of me, because I wouldn't go out with boys. They all said I was a nut case."

When Patti walked down the aisle, Marvin thought, *"Gloria, I wish you could see her, you would be proud. She is beautiful like you. You are completely different. I hope I can learn to lover her like I did you. However, I don't doubt a word she's said. She has never been wrong."*

They were married and everyone thought, *"That Patti knew her peas and cues."* The women all thought, *"That is the most handsome man in Texas. No wonder she waited on him. I would wait ten year, too, for a man like him."*

Mr. Randall wrote a letter to Charlie Thompson. He didn't tell of the wedding, but told Charlie that it may be a year before Marvin returns to Santa Fe, but that he was safe with them and in good hands." Later he wondered if Charlie would read into that, about Marvin being with Patti. He then thought, *"He doesn't even know about Patti."*

They left for New York out of Houston. They caught a passenger ship, and had a suite on the main deck. They loved to stand at the rail and watch the water.

Patti stood very close to Marvin and said the very same words Gloria had said to him, "Do you feel it, Marvin."

"He looked at her and said, "Gloria said those very same words the first day we met. I will tell you what I told her. 'Yes, I do.'"

Patti then put her arms around him and said, "Lord, thank you so much for putting us together," and Marvin squeezed her.

The ship had now rounded Florida and was going up the Virginia shore when they turned into a river. They were eating, and Patti looked at Marvin with a serious look and said, "We need to get off this ship when it docks. She then turned to a passenger sitting at their table and said, "You need to leave with us Mr. Tilley."

He said, "How did you know my name? I haven't used that name in ten years, how did you know it?"

Marvin said, "She gets these feelings, and she's never wrong. If you are wise you will leave with us. Tilley could tell they were serious, and he believed her.

Tilley said, "We need to change into walking clothes and shoes. I'll meet you at the gang plank in ten minutes."

Marvin and Pattie went to their cabin and packed. They had a valise that Marvin packed with essentials. They both put on denim pants and warm shirts. They put on their coats and packed like they were going on a hiking trip. They both had good shoes for walking. Marvin strapped on his colt, and rolled up four blankets and two small pillows. He put his Winchester in the middle, and put ropes around the roll with a loop so Patti could carry it.

Marvin used two straps to make a backpack out of the valise, and they were off. Tilley was waiting for them with a backpack at the gangplank. The first mate was there and said, "You can't get off here, we're just stopping for a passenger."

Marvin didn't even listen to him, and they just pushed past him, and were on the pier. They walked down the pier. There was an Indian in a long boat. Marvin looked at him and said, "We need to get up river in a hurry. The Indian just nodded, and they climbed aboard. The Indian put in four thole pins for the oars, then placed the oars into the pins. Each of them sat at a place, and started rowing. They started up stream. The Indian stood and put up a sail that greatly helped, as the wind had picked up, and they were now moving at a good clip up the river. No one said a word for over an hour. They just rowed in silence.

They continued up the river, and the wind had really begun to pick up. Marvin guessed they were about ten miles up the river, now. The Indian then turned the boat into a creek, and they continued. It was getting dark when the Indian pulled up to a small pier. They all got out, and could see a log cabin up a hill, maybe thirty to forty feet above them. They took all their belongings and headed for the log cabin. After they set their trappings down, the Indian said, "Help me with the boat. I need to sink it or it will wash away.

They went back down to the boat, and the Indian got in the water and pulled one side of it down until the water rushed in it. It then sank to the bottom, but was still tied to the pier.

They returned to the cabin. Marvin could tell it was built by a craftsman, as the logs had been cut to fit perfectly with one another. It had a log roof with slate covering the logs.

The Indian pushed open a massive door that fit snuggly. They all went in, and the Indian lit two candles for light. They placed their things in the room, and returned outside. There was a woodpile that contained about a cord of wood. Tilley and Marvin started toting the wood into the cabin.

The Indian went back into the cabin, and came out carrying an olla that would hold about three gallons of water. Pattie could see what he was doing, and picked up a metal bucket and followed the Indian. They both came back with water. It was now starting to sprinkle.

The Indian began to pull Spanish moss from limbs that nearly touched the ground. Patti saw what he was doing, and followed him. They both brought arm loads of the moss inside, and piled it up. Pattie understood it was for their bedding. By the time they had finished this chore, Marvin and Tilley had all the wood in the cabin.

Marvin noticed that the floor of the cabin was raised, and had a slate floor that fit perfectly to one another. Marvin closed the door just as a torrential rain began to pour. As he closed the door he noticed a rain barrel outside, that had a gutter running from the roof to it.

No one had said a word. They all just functioned. There was a perfectly made fireplace, that had a grill and an iron arm that swung out to cook on. There was a small counter that the Indian had sat his pack on. Marvin noticed pots and pans hanging from the wall, and eating utensils and cups on a rack above the counter. The Indian was now making a stew. While he did this, Patti saw a coffee pot and found a sack of coffee on the counter. She used some water from the olla and made coffee.

By now the wind was howling like crazy. They could tell that a hurricane had blown in. Each wondered about the ship they had been on.

Tilley broke the silence and asked, "How did you know my name?"

Patti said, "I don't know, but you used to go by John Tilley when you were in Missouri. Things just come to me. A voice just told me that you needed me to tell you that bad things were about to happen, and you were important to us."

Tilley said, "I was run out of Missouri by a posse that was going to hang me. I had been badgered into a fight by a man. He tripped over something as we came together, and fell backwards. He hit his head on a rock, and it killed him. He was local, and well liked. They charged me with murder, and

I had nothing to do with it. It was just a horrible accident. I could see some men coming with a rope, so I caught up the nearest horse and got out of there.

"I went to Houston and changed my name. I worked there for ten years, and saved enough money to get to New York. I have a job waiting there for me on Wall Street. I know you had no knowledge of this. I have heard of people like you. God gives them a special talent. I spoke to a man who had that gift. He said it was a curse, and wished he didn't have it."

"Patti said, "I believe God gave me this gift, and I will honor him with it."

"You have a wonderful wife, "Mr. Ellis."

The third day the storm let up and it cleared off. The water was still halfway up the hill. The Indian dived into the water and disappeared. In just a few seconds, they saw him surface with the rope tied to the boat. He swam toward them. They took the rope, and helped pull the boat to them. It was still under water, but the gunnels were now out of the water. The Indian took the metal bucket, and began bailing water out of the boat. Marvin relieved him, then Tilley relieved him. In an hour they had the boat free of water. They then went and collected their things, and put them in the boat. The Indian put in the thole pins, and they all got in the boat and rowed out to the river.

The Indian said, "Nothing will be down river, that all blew away. It has happened before. There will be villages up river. There is a railroad that goes through the village.

CHAPTER 10

More Trouble

KENDALL HENDERSON WAS a major in the confederacy. During the war his family had been killed during Sherman's march to the sea. It turned him bitter. He became an outlaw. For a few years he was a lone bandit. He thought if he involved others, they could cause him to be caught. However, the things he stole didn't amount to much. He knew if he were to take down a bank or a train, he would need a gang.

He started recruiting men for his gang. He was very careful who he recruited. He wanted only those who had been Southern soldiers. He would tell them that what they were doing was not wrong, it was just revenge for what the blue bellies had done to the South.

Kendall carefully planned each robbery. The robberies were much fewer, but the take was much bigger. They were only doing about three robberies a year. He made each man take an oath of silence. No one was to know they were members of a gang. He told his members not to live close to one another. Most had families. To hide their job as an outlaw, the men told their wives they were salesmen, and had to travel at times. They would say they were not connected to any firm, but were freelance salesmen. This covered their large income.

Kendall would do his own scouting and casing of every job. He rarely participated in the robberies, as he was busy planning the next robbery. He told his next in command, who incidentally, had served with him during the war, that if a job looked like something was odd about it, or he thought it may be a trap, to just pull off.

Kendall said, "Howard, it just isn't worth it. There are plenty of safe jobs where no one will get hurt. If they were to catch any of us, it would be all over for all of us." Some of the bank jobs were planned a year ahead of time. They would usually hit a bank just after it opened. The clerks would be laying out the money, and very few people would be on the streets.

Kendall would always have fresh horses for them about ten miles out of town, so if a posse were chasing them, they could just change horses and easily outdistance the posse. In one instance they had two changes of horses, as there were ranches nearby that could give the posse fresh mounts.

The banks they robbed were in different states, and the robberies were generally blamed on other outlaws who had a name, such as the James brothers, the Youngers or others. There was no pattern to their robberies. They held up two trains that Kendall found were carrying an unusual amount of cash.

Kendall lost gang members, who weren't really outlaws, as they just wanted to get a good start to a legitimate living. He now had some very unsavory characters, as another gang of outlaws had lost their leader, and asked to join up with him.

Kendall paid for information, and knew several people in the financial business. These people would get a very large slice of the take. One man told Kendall about a train that was carrying some of the confederate gold from Richmond to Washington. It had been kept in Richmond for several years, but was now needed. There had been a downturn in the economy, and the secretary of the treasure needed it. It was to be transported by train. The train was a short train with one car that had fifteen United States Marshals. Only a handful of people would be leaving at night, and they made the train look like just a local run. The marshals were dressed in civilian clothes posing as passengers. However, no one else was allowed in their car. The other passenger car had seven young women attending a convention in Washington DC and three nuns.

Kendall knew about the deputy marshals, and had a plan for them. Howard was to put ether into the vent from the ceiling. Two others were to lock the doors from the outside so if the ether failed, the deputies could not get out. Just past the James River, the train would stop to take on water. It was a sweet plan.

They would blow the door of the baggage car, and throw smoke bombs into the car. They would then unload the gold and transfer it to long boats that Kendall had hired on the pretence of taking some iron equipment up river. The gold would then be put on wagons, then transferred to Kendall's hideout.

After loading the long boats, the gang would ride off like

they had the gold, then scatter. They were all to meet a month later at the hideout to get their share of the take.

Kendall would only tell his men about the job they were going to do the day before. He now had a very vicious gang. He had kept them in an abandoned house for over a month without liquor or women. They were chomping at the bit.

The robbery went like it was planned. Two of the men were to be at each end of the passenger car to make sure no one would get brave and try to shoot.

***

The Indian had taken them to the railroad, and they had paid him. They then waited for the train. It pulled up and stopped for water. Marvin told the conductor that they would like to board the train and ride into Washington DC. The conductor put them in seats near the end of the coach.

They had only sat there for a few minutes when all the action began. When they heard the noise from the dynamite blowing the baggage car door, both Tilley and Marvin knew immediately that it was a train robbery. Marvin said, "Just stay seated and we will hide our guns, by putting them behind us in our belt. We won't do anything unless we can see our lives being threatened."

The gang transferred the money to the boats, but the two members who were guarding the coach where the young women were, spread the word about the women. So, instead of riding away, they interred the car, and began raping the women. Two of the nuns were stripped of their habits leaving them bare to the waist.

The two men who were supposed to be making sure no one pulled a gun were busy watching the rapes. Marvin and Tilley stood, drew their weapons. They shot both the guards. The gang was caught unaware, and the shooting filled the car with smoke. Both Tilley and Marvin emptied their guns, but Marvin had another gun, and began firing it. They killed seven men of the bandits, before the others scooted out the car and rode away.

The women were all crying and Patti helped the women dress. Inadvertently, three women were shot. Two of them died, and the other was badly wounded. By now the deputies had broken the doors down, and came to the car that carried the women. The women were so hysterical, they didn't know what had happened. Tilley and Marvin were both arrested and taken to Richmond. They and Pattie tried to explain what happened. The deputies not wanting to show how they had been duped, proudly told how they had killed seven of the bandits, and captured two of them. All the deputies got together. The leader said, "If any of us tells what really happened, we will all lose our jobs."

No one would listen to Marvin and John. Patti carried their money as Marvin had given her all the money when the trouble began. She hired a sharp lawyer, and at the trial he explained what had really happened. As the trial had come up quickly their lawyer only found three of the women. These women testified that Tilley and Marvin had shot and killed the bandits before the deputies arrived.

The deputies all swore they had killed the bandits, and that Marvin and Tilley were part of the gang. However, the conductor testified that they were passengers in the car before the robbery occurred.

The prosecuting attorney said they were planted their by the gang. Patti testified that they were on ship named the *Belmont*. The prosecuting attorney said, "The *Belmont* sank during the hurricane, and there were no survivors." This was the first they had heard of the ship's sinking.

As both sides were at a stalemate the judge gave Tilley and Marvin five years for incidental manslaughter. They appealed their case, and this time their lawyer had all the women, who survived, and the three nuns testify that had it not been for these two brave men stopping the rape, they might have all been killed. All said, the deputies did not show up until the bandits had left.

The fifteen deputies still swore they had stopped the bandits themselves, and had disarmed these two bandits. The judge lowered their sentence to one year for obstructing justice. Nothing could be done now, and they were sent to the prison near Richmond.

CHAPTER 11

Prison and Tragedy

PRISON WAS TOUGH. They worked them ten hours a day, six days a week. The food was just enough to keep them alive. Their cells were filthy and infested with fleas and lice. Tilley was put in another part of the prison, as they didn't want them together. They did get together when they were in the prison yard.

Marvin's cellmate was in for armed robbery. He kept bragging about all the jobs he had pulled, and how luxuriously he had live. Marvin never said a word, but his cellmate just talked on and on.

Tilley was rooming with a murderer. He liked to hurt people. Tilley tried to just be passive and do his time, but his cellmate kept badgering him until they got into a fight. His cellmate had a knife, and killed Tilley. Marvin didn't hear about it for another day. He was in the prison yard, and kept to himself. He tried to find Tilley, and then was told about his death.

Marvin found out who killed him. He made sure he was never around him. He did find out who the murderers new cellmate was. He caught him alone and told him he heard that his cellmate had planned to kill him. The new man had several friends. One day there was a gathering around the murderer and a knife was put in him.

Marvin saw it, and went to him acting as if he were trying to help him. He covertly said, "Tilley had this done to you, and if you live, he will have it done again." However, the man died.

Marvin was let out a year later. He wanted to go home, but thought he would try to do something about the deputies who had lied. Another reason was that he only weighed a hundred and thirty-five pounds, and wanted to look good before Patti saw him.

When he was released from prison he wrote Charlie and told him about his weight, and wanted to look good before he came home. Charlie set up a bank account in Richmond for him, so that he now had plenty of money.

Marvin applied and secured a job as a guard with a security company. He met a Pinkerton man his same age, named Paul Mentor. They became close friends. Marvin never told him about his trouble. He just told him about running cattle in the New Mexican Territory. Marvin was quiet while Paul was loquacious, so he was never asked many questions about his life.

Paul had an ailment that was life threatening. His folks lived in Maine, so he left to go back there to address his illness. Paul looked similar to Marvin, so Marvin got the idea of changing identities with him. He applied for a deputy sheriff job using Paul Mentor's name, and got it. He was very good at what he did, and was put on several cases that he solved.

At times, he worked with the U. S. Marshal's office. Slowly, he acquired the names of all the deputies who had lied about him. He found that three of them had quit the marshaling service and had left the state. He found out where they had gone and eventually got their new addresses. He decided to correspond with them by using his new identity. He gave them his post office box as a return address.

He wrote the one deputy, named Herb Curly. He told Herb that the case, where they lied about the two men, was being reopened He said one of the deputies had become religious, and wanted to clear his conscious.

He wrote the other two the same letter. He immediately got responses from all three asking what they should do.

He wrote them that because the case was about to break open, that they should write the new U. S. Marshal and tell him that they just went along with the leader, as he said they may lose their jobs and be prosecuted for dereliction of duty.

The U. S. Marshal took the letters to the prosecutor and asked, "Did you have anything to do with this?"

After convincing the marshal that he didn't, the prosecutor read all three letters of the three ex-deputies confessing to the lies they had told, and telling how they were intimidated into lying about the two men. All the other deputies were then brought in separately, They were warned that if they contacted any of the others, they would probably go to prison. The prosecutor also told them, that if they lied, they would be prosecuted for perjury. In the end, all but two of them, confessed that the leader had concocted the idea, and they just went along with it.

All the deputies, who confessed that they had lied, were

given a year in the penitentiary. The two who stuck to their stories were given seven years. The leader was given ten years. It was headlines in the paper just like the first trial had been. Marvin contacted his lawyer and asked what he should do.

The lawyer said, "I've already asked permission to sue the United States Marshal Service. I've received permission to sue. I didn't want to contact you before I received permission. They will settle out of court, as they surely don't want anymore headlines like a trial would bring. I think you will get a hundred thousand dollars. I will take ten per cent for my effort, if that is okay with you."

Marvin grinned and said, "Ninety thousand will have to do, but I wouldn't serve a year in that prison for twenty-million."

It was six months before Marvin received the money. He decided to use the ninety thousand to take Patti on a trip of a lifetime. He wired her to meet him in New York City at the Metropolitan Hotel. Ten days later Patti arrived. There was a tearful reunion, then he took her on a shopping spree. She protested at the price of several dresses and gowns, but Marvin just bought them anyway. He booked passage on the finest ship line, and they were in the finest first class suite.

When they arrived in London, they stayed at the finest hotel available. There Marvin contacted a tour-guide service. A desk clerk at the hotel put him onto this service. They were impressed by their tour-guide, Paul Devers. He was a man in his fifties, and was highly educated in the history of London.

Marvin said, "Mr. Devers, I want you to work for us exclusively. I want you to dine with us, and be with us twelve hours a day. Can you do that?"

"What you ask will be expensive as I generally have a group."

"I will pay the bill, this is a once in a lifetime trip."

"They toured for ten days. Paul was delightful. He also liked them very much and as Patti said, "I think he enjoyed the tour as much as we did.""

They told Paul about touring Paris. Paul said, "I know just who you should have as a guide there. I went to college with her. We were very close, but it didn't turn out that way, as she married another and I did, too. However, we still write each other. Our spouses put up with it, as we are in different cities, and never see one another. You will love Lisa."

He was right, Lisa was as good as Paul. He had written her on what the Ellis' liked and she did just what Paul had done. She dined with them, and was with them twelve hours a day.

At the end of the tour, she had mapped out where they should go in Europe, and put them onto several other agencies. The trip was marvelous and took six months. At the end they returned to New York City, and then back to Santa Fe. On their way, they decided to visit Patti's parents in Marble Falls.

They were very glad to see them. Actually Patti wanted to tell her parents about their trip. She told every detail, and in the end said, "It was the best honeymoon in the world. Of course it was nearly two years late, but just as good as if it was the day after the wedding."

When J. W. and Mildred were in their bedroom that night, Mildred said, "Patti is the happiest bride I have ever known. She worships Marvin." She then looked at J. W. and added, "I guess we all do. I didn't think I could love someone as much as Chad, but Marvin is pretty close."

J. W. said, "Yes, I think other than making Patti happy, I wanted him as a son. I still miss Chad, but Marvin is like you say, pretty close."

Marvin and Patti had to go back to Austin to catch a train north to Ft. Worth. From there, they bought tickets on a train that would eventually get them to Santa Fe. The train didn't leave until the following morning, so Marvin took Patti to a fine hotel.

They were told that there would be entertainment that night in the ballroom of the hotel. Marvin purchased tickets to the show. It was splendid and Patti said, "I have never been this happy in my life."

They were about to leave when two men got into an argument over a lady. One drew his gun, and the other followed suit. One shot the other dead, but as the one shot was falling, he fired his gun. The bullet hit Patti dead center and she crumbled. Marvin caught her.

A doctor was there and told Marvin to take her to his office, which was right down the street. They were there in less than five minutes, and the doctor already had his coat off as Marvin put her on a gurney he had there. The doctor's wife was already heating water, as the doctor washed up. He then took the clothes off Patti from the waist up. The bullet had hit her dead center.

"He doctor looked at Marvin and said, "She has a chance if the bullet missed her heart. He used his scalpel to cut into her chest. Marvin had to turn away as he could not bear to see Patti cut.

The doctor's wife caught him and said, "Hold me tightly, and don't look. My husband is the best surgeon in the country.

He must have taken thousands of bullets out of soldiers during the war. If anyone can save her, it will be Everett."

Marvin held onto her like she was his mother. He cried, and she patted him.

In about fifteen minutes the doctor said, "I removed the bullet with my forceps. It may have grazed the heart, but didn't penetrate it. She has a chance."

Marvin yelled, "Thank you God!" But still held onto the doctor's wife The doctor was now tying off some bleeders and then sewed her up.

He turned to Marvin and said, "She's now in the hand's of the Almighty. I've seen soldiers with that same kind of wound many times. Some lived and some died. She's strong, and has a chance."

The doctor was washing up, and his wife broke from Marvin, and brought Everett a towel. She said, "Everett always has a drink of brandy after an operation. Just one drink. He says he's celebrating what God has taught him. Will you have a drink with him, Mr. Ellis?"

Marvin had calmed himself, but just nodded. When they were seated next to the table where Patti was, Marvin said, "Thank you so much, doctor. He then turned and said, "Thank you also, Mrs. Brown. You could never know the comfort you gave me. I felt I was in my mother's arms. I cried like I did when I was a kid."

"And rightfully so, Mr. Ellis. We both could feel the love you have for Patti."

They sat there for about a half hour, all looking at Patti. Her eyes blinked and she said, "What happened? I have a pain in my chest," and started her hand toward the wound, but Doctor Brown caught her hand and said, "You were shot Mrs. Ellis, but I have removed the bullet. Now you must do your part and get well.

"Your husband is here with you." Marvin stood and said, "Patti, Doctor Brown has told me you're strong, and can survive this, but you have to try."

Patti smiled and said, "I'll do my best, Marvin, but if I don't make it, just know that I had a marvelous life. No one could love me as much as you do. If I don't make it, take me back to momma and daddy. They'll want to see me for the last time."

Doctor Brown said, "Try to sleep now. Sleep is the best medicine."

Patti closed her eyes, and appeared to go to sleep. They all just sat there and watched her.

Marvin said, "Why don't you two get some rest. If anything changes, I'll come get you."

The Browns left and Marvin scooted his chair closer, and held Patti's hand. He sat their about an hour, then Patti's eyes opened. She looked at Marvin and said, "I'm going home with Jesus, now, Marvin. I saw a bright light, and I know Jesus is coming for me. Just know I am with him, now."

She closed her eyes and went with Jesus.

Marvin knew she was gone, and sat there and cried and cried. Mrs. Brown heard him crying, and started to get up, but Everett pulled her back and said, "He needs to be alone with her now, Martha. Just let him be for awhile, then we'll go to him."

They both dressed, and washed up some. They then

went in as Marvin was calmer now. He looked up with tears running down his face and said, "She told me she was going with Jesus, now, and left us."

Martha said, "She's where we all want to be, Mr. Ellis. She then came to him and pulled him to her, and hugged him tightly. Marvin clung to her for sometime.

He then said, "Where is there a mortician, Doctor Brown?" When Patti was at the mortician office, Marvin said, "I have to take her to her folks near Austin. Do what you have to do, then put her in the finest casket you have. I'll make arrangements with the railroad."

At Austin, Marvin bought a wagon and two mules. They loaded Patti onto the wagon and he headed for Marble Falls. As he approached the ranch, one of the hands spotted him and knew it was Marvin. He turned his horse and rode hell bent for the ranch house. He yelled, "Mr. Randall come quick!"

J. W. and Mildred came to the porch as Marvin pulled up in the wagon. They could both see the coffin. Mildred went to her knees and with her hands outstretched to heaven, yelling, "No, Lord! Not our Patti!"

"J. W., with a grim face said, "What happened, Marvin?"

"We were at a show in Ft. Worth, where two men got into an argument. They drew on one another, and a stray bullet hit Patti dead center. She lived long enough to tell me to take her back to you. She smiled then and said, 'I see a bright light. Jesus is coming for me.' She then went with Jesus."

J. W. picked up Mildred and said, "It ain't right that our children go home before we do, Mildred."

Mildred had recovered and said, "Don't question the Lord, J. W., the Lord giveth and the Lord taketh away." She smiled then and said, "She's with Chad, now. Oh, how I wished I could see them embrace each other. They loved each other so much."

Some of the cowhands had rode up, and all knew that Patti was in the casket. Two of them cried openly.

J. W. then said, "Help me take her to the dining room, boys. I want her on the dining room table. We'll open the casket then, and say our goodbyes."

After the casket was open the boys filed by. All of them had tears running down their faces. Marvin thought, *"She touched them all. I was just lucky enough to have her love for awhile."*

The boys left, and the three of them stood looking at Patti. Mildred said, "She looks so peaceful, like she's just asleep."

J. W. said, "She's the prettiest women in the world with the sweetest heart that every lived."

The funeral was held two days later. Everyone in the county came and filed by to see Patti for the last time.

The minister who married them, gave the eulogy. She was buried on the ranch. Marvin stayed two more days then went back to Santa Fe.

He went directly to Charlie Thomson's office, and told him. Charlie said, "We are very unlucky with women, Marvin. I don't think I will ever go with another. Let's bring your girls to my house, and all of us can live together. You can sell Cordova's place."

"No, I want to hang onto that place. Patti and I were so happy there. I can't live there for awhile, but I know I'll want to live there again. I do like your idea about moving the twins here. We can be co-daddies."

Charlie smiled and said, "I would really like that.

The girls were ecstatic about living with both Charlie and Marvin. They were now teenagers, and both had a crush on both Charlie and Marvin.

CHAPTER 12

Adele Escapes

ADELE WAS TAKEN to the newly opened prison for women in Jefferson City, Missouri. The warden, Avery Johnson, was a man with a penchant for beautiful women. The woman who was in charge of the section that oversaw the dangerous women criminals was named Alma Greg. Avery had seen the lust in Alma's eyes when they were with a very young woman who had just arrived at the prison. He took note of this, and called Alma into his office.

Alma arrived, and Avery closed the door, and told her to have a seat. Alma was in a quandary why the warden would want to see her.

Avery said, "Alma, I think we both have a similar interest, whereby we could help one another."

Alma had a puzzling look on her face, so Avery decided to just come out with it. He said, "I noticed you looking at Patsy Lovett, as she came into the prison. As she is just serving one year for abetting a robbery, I can have her reassigned to your section, and put into a private holding cell. This will give you a time to work your charms on her, and tell her how you can make life easier in return for certain favors.

"I also have a need for good looking women, and you can help me with that. Do you think we could work together to the benefit of us both?"

Alma said, "I think we can, but we must be very careful about how we go about it."

Avery said, "I'll talk to your quarry, and you can talk to mine. We can both explain the facts of prison life to them without anyone, outside of us, being the wiser. If they are uncooperative, we can both explain what can happen to them if they don't take our offer.

"In the case of Miss Lovett, I will tell her I will assign her to be a cellmate of a large lesbian, who she will not like at all, or she can live by herself in a private cell and meet a person who will care for her, and make her life here enjoyable.

"When I see someone I want, you can tell her much the same story. Tell her you have an "in" with the warden, and he can make her life very nice if she will be kind to him. Do we have a deal?"

"Sounds good to me, Warden. I want that Lovett girl. Can you talk to her today?"

"Sure. Tell Howard that I need to interview her, and to send her up. If she is intelligent, she will be transferred to that private cell at eight tonight. That will give you time to fix up her cell nicely, then be alone with her later."

Patsy was sent to the warden's office and he said, "Patsy, prison life can be as hard or nice as you want it. If you do certain favors for people, it can be very nice for you. Your meals will be private, and you won't have to eat the swill they serve to the others. You can have wine with your meals, and eat as well as you would like. You can sleep on a nicer bed and have any books you want, and other conveniences that other prisoners have no privy to."

"What do I have to do?"

"There is a woman who works here who likes you very much. If you will be nice to her, she can make your year here easy."

Patsy said, "And if I don't, you will make things tough for me."

"Not us, but you will probably be put with a large woman who will have you do what she wants. If you refuse, she will like that even better. No matter, you will give her what she wants. What will it be?"

"The easy way, I suppose."

She was very good to Alma, because she knew if she wasn't, it would be terrible for her.

Alma and Avery worked together nicely. Each tired of their women fairly quickly, but even though their quarries were sent back to the regular prison cells, they saw to it, that they had nice cellmates.

When Adele came to the prison, Alma spotted her. She was too old for Alma, as she liked her girls to be young, but she knew the warden would like her. After Adele had checked in, Alma had her brought to her office. She said, "Adele, prison can be what you make it. Here we have a warden who enjoys the finer things in life. If you want it easy here, be nice to him."

"You mean if I bed him, I will get special treatment."

"That's a little cruder than I would have put it. The warden is a nice looking man, but he's lonely. He's married to a cold woman and needs warmth. Do you think you could make him happy?"

"I've made many men happy, what's one more?"

"Then we have an understanding."

"Yes."

The first meeting with the warden went nicely. Adele had a way about her to make men adore her if she wanted them. She turned on all her charm to the warden, and he began to fall in love with her. She could see this, and worked it to the maximum. Within the year she had him hopelessly in love with her.

They began to think of ways to get her out of the prison. She told him, "I was married to a very wealthy man. You can check on that if you want. His name is Charles Thompson, and he lives in Santa Fe. Through the years I acted like I spent a lot of money, but I was rat holing most of it so I could get away from him. He couldn't satisfy me like you do.

"I have twenty-thousand dollars in cash hidden away. We could get away from here and live in luxury. There are places in Mexico where we could live a dream life. However, we must find a way to get me out of here. I think the best way would be to have an explosion where someone was blown up. You could tell everyone I was lost in the explosion.

"However, you may have a better plan. You could say I escaped, and put them on a wrong trail, then meet me in Mexico about six weeks later. You could take a vacation, and then have it reported that you were lost at sea. You have to plan it, as I'm confined."

The escape seemed better to Avery. He so wanted Adele.

She was everything he ever dreamed about. He kept her away from the other women, because he knew eventually, they would turn her to liking women as most did. He had seen it with another woman that he liked very much.

He set the escape up by bribing a doctor who was a dope addict. The doctor said Adele had to have an operation by a specialist. She was taken with Alma as the guard, and the doctor to another hospital. They explained later, that somehow Adele got possession of a gun, and forced them to take her to a train heading to Kansas City. She had a change of clothes, so someone must have aided her.

Adele actually got onto the train, and purchased a ticket from the conductor, but then got off a few minutes later. Avery met her and drove her back where she caught the train to St. Louis. From there she boarded a riverboat going to New Orleans. There, she caught another ship heading for Mexico.

Avery had given her a thousand dollars. She had given him the name of a place in Acapulco to meet her in six weeks. He had planned a vacation for then. It looked iron-clad. However, six weeks later, he went to Acapulco, and there was no Adele. It took him to the end of his vacation to realize he had been duped.

Adele went back to Virginia. Before she had left for Santa Fe, she had met a Clarence Dowd and his wife at the Governor's ball. She found that they were very wealthy. She had kept this in the back of her mind for future reference. When she returned to Virginia, she met them again at a party. She danced with Clarence, and danced close to him. He was smitten. She then planned an accident for his wife. Adele had invited them to her house for a dinner. After dinner they had some sherry. She had planted some knockout drops in the wife's drink. She then asked Clarence to go to the kitchen, and get a bottle that she could not reach, as it was on her top shelf. The wife nodded off. Adele took a small pillow and held it over her mouth and nose until she was out forever. Clarence was in the kitchen still trying to get the bottle, when Adele came and said, "Your wife seems to have gone to sleep."

Clarence said, "She never could hold her liqueur. Let's just lay her on your sofa. She'll come around in a minute or two. They waited, and an hour later, they checked on her. She was dead. They called a doctor and he said, "She must have had a heart attack. Adele was with him at the funeral, and helped him.

They met again a month later at a party and danced together. Again Adele danced close, and put her leg between his. He was excited. They met then a few times, but Adele wouldn't bed him. This just made him want her all the more.

Adele said, "We can never be together here, as people know she died at my house.

If we are to be together, we must go away. I suggest Europe. It will take a lot of money, and I don't have much.

Clarence said, "I have enough, I can tell you."

"It's hard to exchange money in America," Adele mentioned, "I suggest we take a great deal in cash, then change it when we get to Europe."

Adele made the arrangements. They would go to Bermuda first, then on to London.

On the way to Bermuda, Adele gave him the best love he had ever had. He was hopelessly in love with her. The second night she asked him to take her to the stern of the ship to get some air. When they arrived, there was no one around.

Adele kept leaning over the railing looking down. Clarence asked, "What are you looking at, Adele?"

Adele said, "It's a mysterious glow."

Clarence looked, but couldn't see it. She said, "Stand on your tiptoes, and look straight down."

He said, "I still can't see it."

She said, "Let me help you," and she went behind him and picked him up. As she did, she raised him up enough to lift him over the railing.

She waited another few minutes, then ran to an officer on the ship. She excitedly told him that her husband had fallen overboard. The officer went to the captain, but the captain said, "It would be of no use to turn around. We could never find him in the dark. Besides, from that height he would be unconscious and go down. I'm sorry, but there is nothing to do. It has happened before."

When Adele returned to her cabin, she put all his money in her valise and everything else he had of value. The next day, she went to the captain and asked if she would be compensated by the ship lines. She said she saw it as their fault for not having higher railings.

She told the captain that she would be debarking at Bermuda, as her trip was ruined. She said, "I will be waiting there for the compensation."

Adele wept and said, "I need you to help me, Captain." She was now leaning on him and clutching him. He liked that, and told her he would go with her to the claims office.

She dined each night with him, and held to him like he was her protector.

However, He had to sail with his ship, and they parted. The next week she was notified that her claim had been processed. The ship line paid her twenty-five thousand dollars.

Adele had met a couple from England who were going to Mexico. Adele asked if they were going to visit Acapulco. They said they were. She asked if they would post a letter for her while they were there. They agreed, so she wrote Avery at the prison. She said she had waited over three months, wondering when he were coming. She said that she had run up so many bills that she had to skip out before they put her in jail. She asked him to send her another thousand dollars.

Adele wrote, "I have missed you so much, I can hardly stand it. She wrote please send the money, to Petersburg, Virginia, general delivery. I will then have money to meet you in Denver at the Cow Palace," and gave him a date.

Avery thought, "I must have missed her somehow in Acapulco. He was awash with love again, and that night mailed her a check for a thousand dollars.

She had arrived in Virginia, and went to Petersburg. The check was waiting for her. She cashed it and left for Alexandria. As she traveled she thought, *What an idiot that Avery is.*

That night she had an erotic dream about Marvin. He was a handsome man. She wondered why he had refused her. No man had ever done that. She tried to count how many men she had bedded, but she couldn't remember all of them. She began thinking how she may get money from Charlie. She knew that of all the men she had known, he loved her the most. She could get anything from him.

She thought if she waited another five years or more, Charlie would remarry. If he did, she may be able to blackmail him.

She then thought of Marvin, and wondered if he had anything to do with exposing her. She decided that he probably did, as his wife wouldn't have been secretive about her dealings with the Truan Detective Agency. He needed to be taught a lesson, however, that would have to wait. As she thought, she knew she would have to wait five or ten years, and then pay him a visit that he would not soon forget.

Adele had a lot of fun thinking what she would do to him. The best thing would be to have two men abduct him and tie him to a bed, naked. She would then have her pleasure with him.

He would probably be married again, and she would hire some one to take pictures of her making love to him while he was tied. She would then send the pictures to his wife.

She also thought of the detective, Glenn Truan. He needed to be taught a lesson, also. She would somehow have him drugged, then have prostitutes be with him while she took picture to send to his wife.

She traveled to New Orleans, and decided to stay there awhile. She was a master at getting invited to places. Soon she integrated with the society there. She met a man, Wade Herman, who was very rich. He was about sixty.

She was dancing with him and meshed her body to his, so she could get him excited. As she danced close she put her lips to his neck. Soon he was panting and she knew she had him. He asked her if she was a widow, and she said she was.

She then, through some tears, told how her husband had fell overboard while they were sailing to Europe.

Although he was married, she soon was bedding him. She had made friends with a broke reporter who was always looking for news. She told him that she would set up Herman. The reporter would burst into the room with his camera while they were making love. With the pictures, they could blackmail him. She anonymously sent the photos to his business and soon had ten thousand dollars. She gave the reporter five-hundred, and told him she was splitting the blackmail money with him, as the man was nearly broke and could only afford a thousand.

It was now six years since she had escaped from the state prison. She traveled more now, as she didn't like to stay anyplace very long.

She felt it was safe now, so she went to Denver. She had visions of exacting her revenge on Marvin, Glenn Truan and maybe even Charlie. Unbeknown to her, Brodie was at a restaurant where she was eating. He noticed her and wired Marvin.

The wire said:

I SPOTTED ADELE THOMPSON IN DENVER STOP SHE IS STAYING AT THE COW PALACE STOP PLEASE ADVISE, BRODIE STOP

Marvin wired back that he should go to the local police and have her arrested. The local police picked her up, and she was taken back to Jefferson City Prison.

She arrived and Alma met her when she came in. Alma

said, "You bilked the warden out of a lot of money. He will probably want to punished you. However, if you have some money, I can probably see that you don't suffer too, badly. How about it?"

"I have several thousand dollars in a bank account. We can probably do business I surely don't want to stay here. If you can get me out of here, I can make it worth your while."

"Talk is cheap, Thompson. I need to see the color of your money."

"I can't do anything from here. You will have to trust me."

"Like Avery trusted you? I don't think so. I've got a roommate lined up for you. Her name is Norma Anderson. She's well over six feet tall and weighs about two-fifty. She loves it when you struggle. I told her about you, and she said she was looking forward to you giving her what she likes. You'll do it too, after a little persuasion. She's not stingy, though, and will probably share you with some of her friends."

"So, what must I do to get out of that?"

"Have a thousand dollars transferred to my bank account. All the mail is monitored, so you will have to send a letter by me."

"The bank won't transfer money unless I'm there in person. I have several thousand, and if you get me out of here, I'll give you a thousand. You will have to earn it, Alma."

"I'll see what I can do, but Avery will want to see you. I can't stop him if he decides to punish you. You better be thinking of what you're going to tell him. I know he won't go along with any scheme of getting you out of here. Twice burned, you'll find him a little harder to deal with. Besides he has a new woman, now."

CHAPTER 13

Another Excape then Scams

W HEN AVERY SAW her, he had an evil smile on his face. He said, "Welcome home Adele. I've got a surprise for you. You're going to love it. Alma and I have talked and think you will enjoy your new cellmate, Norma Anderson. She will show you another side of love life.

"However, I'm not sadistic. I will move you around a lot, so you can know, in the Biblical sense, a lot of women. Alma will probably have them bid for you."

"I know you think me terrible, Avery, but you would have to know the circumstance. I don't know how we missed each other in Acapulco, and on the way to Denver, I was spotted by someone who tipped off the authorities. When I reached Denver I was arrested. I've always loved you Avery, and you know it."

"Yes, you always loved me and probably a lot of others. I can't believe you anymore, Adele. You've burned me for the last time."

"You know you love me Avery. We would be good together."

"Yes, if we ever got together. I have a new love, now, and she has put no demands on me. She gets out in two months, though. If Norma doesn't turn you into a lesbian, maybe I will see you then."

"If you do that to me, Avery, I could never love you again."

"Oh, I think you will. After a couple of weeks with Norma, you may be a lot more willing."

Adele was taken by a guard to Alma's office again. Alma said, "You can see, now, how disappointed Avery was. I've been thinking. I may be able to get you out of here, but I will have to know a lot more about your money. You will have to send the bank a note that you want an accounting. I'll set up a P. O. box in Jefferson City, and you can have the accounting sent to that post office box. That way I'll know if you are on the up and up."

"I can do that. Give me a pen and paper." In a few minutes Adele scratched out a letter to the First Bank of Denver. She asked for an accounting of her savings account. She had several accounts in several cities, so that no one would know the extent of her wealth. At the Denver bank, she had five thousand dollars.

Adele then said, "You'll never get a cent if you put me with those women, so think about it."

Alma smiled and said, "I can put you in a holding cell by yourself, until we get an answer from your bank.

Adele was kept away from the others in a holding cell. A couple of weeks later, a smiling Alma came to her cell and said, "I see you weren't lying to me, Adele. You have a little over five-thousand there."

"Well, what are you going to do about it."

"I've been thinking. The medical scheme won't work anymore, as the warden has to approve that, and I'm sure he won't be burned again. We do have groceries delivered every Wednesday. Three wagons come here from Jefferson City.

"You'll have to be in the yard when they arrive. I can keep you here in a holding cell until the wagons get here. When the time is right, I will have a guard walk you to the door leading to the yard. I've done some favors for that guard, and she will do anything I ask. I will have her leave you by that door. You can peer out and see when Paco has the his wagon ready for you. You will then go and get into the space Paco will provided for you. No one can see you. The guard can say she brought you to the yard for exercise, then left, once you were in the yard. Paco is good at having a space that when they search his wagon, they won't find the space. I've used Paco to smuggle in contraband before. I will go over with you on exactly what you have to do. I can easily bribe Paco. He's a Mexican, who has a grudge against the prison. He thinks they cheated him out of some money. I'll tell him I'll go through the system, and get his back pay with interest. He will think I'm a good guy. I'll then tell him that I need him to smuggle you out. I'll promise him that I will stand up for him if anyone accuses him of helping you.

"The space you will occupy will be on the side of the wagon near the door where you will be standing. No one will see you. Paco will open the space for you, and you can crawl into it. Paco will pull a board down over the space, then lock it in place. It will just look like part of the wagon.

"The wagons comes in well after the time the prisoners go

to the yard. They'll be doing activities, and the guards will be watching them. After the wagons are unload, they search them before they leave. You will be in the back wagon.

"About a half mile away from the prison, I'll have a buggy waiting for you, and take you to a safe place. You will have to wait there a week, as there will be many people looking for you. You will be in a farmer's barn. I'll have it stocked with food. It won't be easy, but in a week, I'll come get you, and we'll leave. I'll be dressed as a man, and you will be dressed as an old lady. We will travel to Kansas City and go from there to Denver on a train. Just remember, I'm much bigger than you, and I'll kill you if I have to."

The day came when Adele was to leave. Paco had his wagon near the door, and in a flash, Adele went into the space and Paco locked the board in place. They left and it seemed like an eternity before Paco pulled up and let her out. Adele was wringing wet from sweat, and gasped for fresh air. A woman was there with a buggy. She instructed Adele to get into the back under a tarp. They drove what seemed an hour to a barn. There was a secret door that gave entrance to a hidden room in the barn. Adele went in, and the buggy pulled away.

Adele lit a lamp, and saw that she had a cot to sleep on. The food was in jars The food was vegetables, fruit and some jerky. She marked off each day, and a week passed. Then she heard a buggy pulling up to the barn. Alma was there wearing a man's suit. She had clothes that old women wore, and Adele put them on. They camped the first night, but the next day they caught the train to Kansas City. All the while, Adele kept a scarf on and wore the old clothes.

They caught another train to Denver. Alma said, "The way we'll make the transfer is that you will write a check to me for the thousand. I will then cash it, and we will part. That way there will be no funny business."

However, Adele had another plan. When they entered the bank, Adele jumped toward a guard and yelled, "That man has a gun, and is going to rob the bank. The guard grabbed Alma's arm and brought his pistol out. Alma was searched, and she had a gun. Being she was dressed in men's clothing, she knew it would take some time to explain that she was a prison guard, and was allowed to carry a gun. Meanwhile, Adele went to the counter and withdrew a thousand dollars. She then walked out and caught the train back to Kansas City.

It took two days for Alma to verify that she was a prison guard at Jefferson's women's prison, and was just on vacation. She said she often dressed in men's clothing as some of the ex-con women were vindictive, and she did it for safety reasons. She said she was in the bank to see if she could cash a check on her account in Jefferson, Missouri.

They let her go, and she returned to Jefferson. She had set up her vacation before Adele's escape, so Avery thought she had nothing to do with the escape. They were still investigating the escape. They had searched the wagons when they came in and left, but could see no way, that Adele could have escaped.

Marvin got the report that Adele was on the loose again. He had paid a guard to keep him notified. He knew how wily Adele could be, and with her looks, she could manipulate people easily.

Marvin decided to pay a detective service to have some one investigate her whereabouts. He knew that Adele was a native of Alexandria, Virginia. He went to Glenn Truan, and asked if the Pinkerton Agency had an office in Alexandria.

Glenn said, "I have a pamphlet with all the offices of the Pinkerton Agencies." he pulled it out of a drawer, and then turned it toward Marvin. "Yes, they do have an office there."

It had an address, so Marvin copied it down and wrote a letter to them with a check of fifty dollars. Two weeks later he received a letter from them, stating that they were now trying to locate Adele Thompson, and would keep him informed. A week later they wrote that they could find no evidence that Adele Thompson was in their area.

What Adele had done, was to locate in Arlington and change her name on her bank accounts and her name as well. She had also altered her looks by buying wigs. They were expensive wigs that fit her well. Even her clothes were different. Whereas she had worn flashy clothes in the past, she now wore conservative clothes.

She decided the best way to meet prominent men was at church. She enjoyed getting them alone, then working them up by teasing them until they were in love with her. She had long ago known that men who were around sixty, were the easiest prey. Their wives no longer gave them the thrill that a younger woman could. She also noticed men who had a wandering eye. They were the easiest.

At the church she attended, she met a couple who were in their late fifties. They were James and Katy Stanton. They owned a large plantation, but had built a townhouse as Katy preferred urban life, now.

Adele had notice James eyeing a young woman as she exited her pew and showed a bare ankle. She then knew she could get him. It was not just the money anymore, she liked the chase, and being bedded by these men. She had found that men in their sixties were better lovers, and she could get them to do anything she wanted. She loved the control the best.

Adele told the Stantons of the loss of her husband in the terrible accident of him falling overboard on their way to Europe. They were both sympathetic. They were having a ball at their town home and asked Adele to attend so she could meet the people.

Adele said, "I have no one to escort me."

Katy said, "I'll send James to pick you up."

Adele couldn't believe how easy this would be. When James arrived for her, she asked him to have cocktail before they left. She said, "It will calm my nerves. I'm very nervous when I meet new people."

She said, "Please help me fix our drinks."

As they went toward the liquor cabinet, Adele slipped, and James caught her. She was in his arms, and put her arms around him and said, "You are so manly. I may have turned my ankle had it not been for your quick action."

They stood with the embrace for a second or two, then had their drinks. As James was helping her in his buggy, she fell against him again and laughed. She said, "I seem to be falling for you, James," Then looked into his eyes as he had his arms about her. She wasn't smiling now, but had a serious look as their eyes locked.

She then said, "You must show me your plantation sometime. I would love to see it with you."

James was hooked. Later that week he sent a message to

her that invited her to see his plantation the next Wednesday. He knew this was the day that Katy chaired a women's group at the church.

As they rode to his plantation, Adele scooted over next to him and said, "Do you mind if I sit close, horses have always scared me."

James smiled and said, "I would enjoy that. The plantation was well organized, and it only took an hour to see all there was to see. He then took her into the plantation manor for a cool drink.

Adele said, "Could we have sherry?"

James had a servant bring them sherry to an upstairs sitting room. He told the servant to leave the bottle, and that she would not be needed anymore.

Adele stood and said, "Let's toast."

James stood and came to her, and they clinked glasses. Their eyes locked and Adele said, "You do something to me that no other man has ever done."

James set their glasses down and came into her arms, and they kissed. He was in love."

Adele said, "How can we be together."

James said, "I will arrange something. Just be patient."

Adele said, "I can't be patient. You have turned my head. I think about you all through the day."

"I'll think of something. It won't take me long."

"Do you ever need to go out of town?"

"Yes. Last year I went to New York City, as I own shares in an office building. I can arrange to have a letter delivered that asks me to attend a meeting of the owners. He then said, "No, that won't work. Katy will want to go."

"How about a hunting trip. I'm sure she wouldn't want to go hunting."

"No. But the hunting season is over. I need to think of something else."

Adele didn't want James to have a quick conquest, so she just teased him. When they kissed, she would rub her body on his, but when he tried to take further liberties, she would stop him and say, not until it's safe." She knew this would make him wild for her.

They did have some time together, as she was staying at the hotel where he had meetings. He would slip away from the meetings and meet her in her room. At one of these meetings Adele said, "I hate to bring this up, but I'm going broke living in this hotel. I need a house. If I could buy a house, I would, but I don't have the money. Could you find it in your heart to buy me one? It doesn't have to be fancy, just comfortable."

"That's a fine idea. Why don't you look for one, and when you find what you want, I'll provide funds for it. Try to get one that has a barn where I wouldn't be seen coming and going."

Adele began to look. She found just the place. It was well built with an expensive interior. It had a lavish bathroom with a large tub and a kerosene water heater. It was also, strategically locate, very close to downtown, and had a barn whose access came off an alley. Large trees surrounded the alley, so no one could see down it unless they happened to be in the alley themselves. The place had a very high price of two thousand dollars. That was what small farms were going for.

The land agent said, "This is a good investment. It sits

right on the edge of the downtown. The town will grow, and with it, the price will increase."

It was just what Adele wanted, but could she persuade James into giving her the two thousand dollars?

At the next opportunity, Adele showed him the house. She said, "It's less than five minutes from the hotel. You could walk. That may be safer anyway, as everyone knows your buggy."

James was very pleased with the house and mostly the location. It had an easy way to get there in secret. She showed him the bath that had a chandelier. She pointed out the large bathtub and said, "It's big enough for two," with a twinkle in her eye.

James could just see he and Adele in that tub together. He then thought of the cost.

He asked, "How much do they want for it?"

Adele said, "It's expensive, but our being together doesn't have a price. Just think. We may be able to be together twice a week or more."

James then repeated, "How much is it?"

She weakly said, "Two thousand dollars."

"My god, that is expensive."

"But it's for us, James. Of course it must be in my name or the assessor would know that you are keeping me."

"I'll have to think this over. I can get the cash, but keeping Katy from finding out will be another thing. Let me give it some thought."

Adele then came into his arms and kissed him. James again let his passion overcome him, but Adele moved away and said, "You should go. Let me know. You can have the money transferred from another bank into my account."

It took some finagling, but James found a way by selling some cattle, then having the buyer put the money in an account in another bank. He then transferred the money to Adele's account without anyone being the wiser.

When Adele received the money she had a decision to make. Just take the money and relocate, or buy the place and have an investment. However, she would then be stuck with James until she could get him caught by his wife.

Adele smiled to herself, *"Katy would not want the embarrassment of that spreading, so she would keep it quiet. Their children and the community would be unaware."*

She then thought, *"This could take months to set up and meanwhile, I would have to put up with James. I am already tired of him, and don't like the thoughts of him sprawling all over me."*

She finally decided to just take the money and relocate. She was becoming bored with James, and she surely didn't want to put up with his pawing and panting. She wrote a letter to him. It was delivered to him personally while he was at a meeting. It read:

My Dearest James,

As deeply as I love you, I could not bring myself to break up your marriage.

The two thousand dollars is only a loan until I'm back on my feet. You can count on me paying you back after I am in California.

I will always keep you near my heart. I wish we could be together, but my conscious will not allow me do it.

I will love you forever,
Adele

She decided to go back to the West. She loved it out there. She wouldn't go to Denver, as too many people could recognize her. She decided to go south of Denver to Colorado Springs. It was a thriving community. It was close enough to Santa Fe to investigate the possibilities of getting revenge on some of the men in Santa Fe. She always thought of Marvin. She wanted him, but she also wanted him to suffer.

She wore her wigs and new clothes and thought no one could recognize her.

CHAPTER 14

Girls to School and Revenge

B ACK IN SANTA Fe, Charlie's and Marvin's ranches were prospering. They had invested in real estate, and that was one of their main businesses. They had hired a smart young man, Gerald Rollins, to run that business. Gerald had come to them and told how he had worked for a land agent in Chicago, but had left when a man named Bill Buchanan had taken over the city. As there were other land dealers in Santa Fe who were established, he knew he had to have a name to back him or he would fail.

Charlie Thomson and Marvin Ellis were very popular, and as one man told Gerald, "They are the toast of Santa Fe." He thought if he could convince them to be his partner, he could use their name, and with his know how, their business would thrive.

He came to them and laid out his proposal. He told of his success in Chicago and why he left. He said, "Without a name it would take me years to make an impact. I have very little money, and I will need a good location and advertisement. You have the funds to furnish that. Together we could really do well here. Santa Fe is growing, and we could grow with it."

They were impressed with the young man and decided to back him. Charlie later said, "That was one of the wisest decisions we ever made.' Gerald was true to them and never tried to back out of their deal. He said, "You put me where I am, and I will never pullout on you."

Both Charlie and Marvin had been asked to run for seats on the city council, as two councilmen had retired. They ran unopposed, and were elected. Everyone knew them, and they were both the most eligible bachelors in Santa Fe.

The twins lived with them and adored them both. They both called Charlie and Marvin by their first names. They were now in high school, and were young women. Every time there was a school function, the girls insisted that Charlie and Marvin be their escorts.

Both men protested and said, "We know the boys ask you, so why don't you go with them?"

Lydia said, "Both Lisa and I are in love with you, and don't want boys."

Charlie looked a Marvin and said, "These girls are crazy. Here we are two old codgers, who may die in a couple of years from old age. Look at the wrinkles on me. Pretty soon I'll be drooling, and you will have to change me like a baby."

Lisa said, "But until that time, we will be with the most handsome men in the country. I just love the looks that our teachers get when they see us with you. They almost turn green."

"Miss Berra asked me if you ever dated. I told her all the

time. She looked interested, and then I said, 'They took us to dinner just two nights ago.'"

Marvin said, "Now that won't do. People will start talking with remarks like that."

Lydia said, "Then you'll have to marry us."

Charlie said, "They have it all mapped out, Marvin. They at least told us about their plans. Now we have to counter that."

"Looks like they're headed for boarding school back East, Charlie."

Lydia said, "You wouldn't do that would you, Marvin?"

"Well, Charlie and I like refined women, and that means that you have to go through a finishing school. We couldn't entertain or go to adult functions with untrained wives. Don't you agree, Charlie?"

"Of course. Next semester you both graduate, and that is where you're headed. Marvin I know just the place."

"We'll go if you will promise to marry us when we graduate. How long is that school?"

"Three years, but you can come home during the summers. We will need you then to help us with the cattle."

"You work us like men, but we both love working cows. When you two get too old to run the businesses, your sweet wives will take over for you."

Marvin and Charlie took them on the train back to New York. There was a good school at Poughkeepsie. Charlie had written the school several months in advance and enrolled the girls. The girls wrote every week and told how much they missed them.

The annual city fiesta was coming up. Each year the city

put on a dance and people brought dishes. The food was terrific and both Charlie and Marvin looked forward to it.

At the dance Miss Berra was near Marvin and said, "I'm glad to see your two daughters are away at school. They are getting to be ladies now. Do you miss them?"

"Yes, they write Charlie and I each week. The only way we got them to go was to promise to marry them after they graduate."

"This shocked Miss Berra and she said, "You don't intend to marry them do you?"

"No, I look at them as my daughters, but like most girls their age, they get a fancy for older men. It's just a phase. After three years, they will see us as we are, old men."

"I don't see you as an old man, how old are you?"

"I'm thirty-four."

"Don't you intend to remarry at some point in your life?"

"I don't worry about it. If someone comes along, it may happen. I was headed for California when I met the girl's mother. I had no intention of marrying. However, when we saw each other, there was no doubt with either of us that we would marry. The girls were six. When their mother was killed, they looked to Charlie and me, and transferred all the love they had for their mother. They now look at us as the love of their lives, but they'll change."

"And if they don't.....?"

Marvin sighed and said, "I guess we'll have to marry them."

Miss Berra said, "Men!" and stomped off.

Charlie was standing close and had heard the conversation.

He said, "Marvin, you have a wonderful way of brushing women off," and they both laughed.

Neither Charlie or Marvin danced much. Some of the wives of the other councilmen dragged them onto the dance floor.

Nancy Craig, a councilmen's wife said, "You need a girlfriend, Marvin."

"You mean since my girlfriend is in college?"

"She laughed and said, "There has been some talk about that. Bob gets a kick out of it. They look just like their mother. She was the prettiest woman I ever saw, and the girls are going to be just as pretty. Bob said that you work them like men. That alone should have made them look forward to college.

"I know you miss Patti, but you need to go on with your life. She was as pretty as Gloria. Where do you find women that pretty.

"I just ran into Gloria, but Patti was different. I worked on this ranch in Marble Falls, Texas and she was the bosses daughter. She was ten years old when I left for California. Like most girls at ten, she had a fantasy of loving an older man. I was ten years older than her when I left. She made me promise to come back and marry her in ten years.

"I came back to see the Randall's after Gloria was killed as I needed them. It was ten years to the day that I left, which was Patti's birthday. Her folks told me that Patti had never gone out with another person after I left. She kept saying I would be back, even though I had never corresponded with them. "Patti was sitting on the front porch in her Sunday best when I rode up. J. W. and Mildred couldn't believe it. Patti just said, "I told you he would be here. I just went along with it and said, 'An Ellis' word is his bond. I didn't realize she meant that I would come back and marry her. However, I knew I could never find a sweeter girl in this world, and if anyone could help me over the sorrow I felt in losing Gloria, it would be Patti. I also wanted to make everyone of the people who had ridiculed her for waiting for me, to eat crow.

"Turned out, I loved her as much as Gloria. Patti had said, that you can love two people. She told me she loved both her mom and dad. It made sense. I also could hear Gloria telling me to go on with my life, just as you just said, Nancy.

"I found two wonderful women, but I don't think there'll be another. I would always compare them to my two wives, and none would measure up."

"Do you think the girls will want to marry you in three years?"

"No. I think they will grow up, and lose the puppy love. Charlie and I had to promise we would marry them, before they left. Once they meet some of those West Point cadets, they will change their minds. When their mother died they just transferred all their love to Charlie and me. They grew up much to fast. I wanted them to stay little girls all their lives."

"Yes, Bob said the same thing about our girls, and now they're both married and have children. It happens too fast."

A single woman was dancing with Charlie. She had her head by his shoulder and Charlie had a pained look on his face. Marvin cut in on him and said, "You're monopolizing all the good looking women, Charlie," and Charlie handed her over with a grateful face. It was at the end of a song, so Marvin took her back to where she was seated. When Marvin returned Charlie said, "Marvin, I like you more everyday," and they both laughed.

***

Adele had hired a man to rent her a house near the edge of Santa Fe. She moved in late one night. She had hired a maid in Colorado Springs who was unattached. Her name was Karen. Karen was widowed, and now at forty needed a job badly. Adele paid her handsomely. She told Karen that she was wanted by the police in Santa Fe for a silly crime. She told her that the man who had her prosecuted needed to be punished.

Adele asked Karen to do all the grocery shopping, and pay the bills like she was the one renting. Karen explained Adele to people by telling them she was not quite right in the head. She said that Adele was her sister. When Adele left the house, she was always with her maid, Karen.

Adele always wore scarves and dark glasses. Karen explained that Adele had a contagious skin disease, so no one came near her. Adele asked Karen to try and find some men who were small time crooks. She found two, Lonnie and Burt. They never had a job, and when they did, they drank up the proceeds quickly.

Adele paid them to meet some local whores. She told them that due to her skin condition she could no longer enjoy sex, but she loved to watch people having sex. She invited them to the house to perform. The women wanted more money for this, and Adele paid it, and Karen watched, also. She always wore her scarves and dark glasses, so no one could recognize her.

A few days later, she asked the men if they wanted to make some big money. Lonnie said, "How big?"

"A hundred dollars each," Adele answered.

Burt said, "Who do we have to kill?" and Adele laughed.

She said, "I want you to drug a man and bring him here, and have your whores make love to him."

"You are weird, lady. Just anyone, or do you have someone in mind?"

"You know that detective, Glenn Truan?"

"Yeah, he got us locked up for a month last year. We hate him."

"I don't know how you'll do it, but I want him here on the bed. I want your whores to work on him, and do all the sex acts they know. I want to photograph them. I collect sex pictures. It's the nearest to sex I can get."

"I'll go to Doc Evers, he's a drug addict. If I give him ten dollars, he'll loan me a hypodermic needle and some knockout drugs. Truan stops for a drink at Murphy's on Friday evening after work. If we catch him as he is going out of Murphy's, we can put the needle in him.

"We can then put him in his buggy and bring him hear." It took a week to line up the girls, get the drug and wait for Truan. He came out of Murphy's just at dusk and Lonnie put the needle in him. Burt had Glenn's buggy ready.

They was at Adele's house five minutes later. The girls were already in place.

Adele had the room well lighted and her camera ready. They stripped Truan and the girls worked on him. They did every sex act they knew, as Adele took pictures. Some of them looked like Glenn was asleep, but some were good. He was coming out of his stupor, now, so he was driven to a seedy hotel, and put in a room with the girls. They undressed him again, and when he regained his consciousness, wanted to know where he was, and why they were all nude.

Thelma said, "You paid us five dollars to do you, Mister. I swear you were really good. You did both of us several times. Anytime you want us again, we're here at the hotel."

Glenn was now getting control, and put on his clothes. Adele and Karen had left at the same time the girls drove Glenn to the hotel. Adele and Karen drove back to Colorado Springs. Adele had learned to develop pictures. Karen was into it now, and enjoyed looking at the pictures. They made several prints, and picked out the best photos.

Adele paid a man from Colorado Springs to deliver the pictures to Lonnie and Burt. They were to deliver the pictures to Glenn's wife during the day when Glenn was at work.

When Glenn came home that night his wife had the pictures laying on the dining room table. She had sent their children over to Glenn's brother's house.

Glenn looked at the pictures and said, "That's Adele's work. They drugged me and I woke in the Jackson hotel with those women. They said I had hired them, but I didn't. I was drugged and was mostly unconscious. Just look at the pictures closely.

His wife picked them up, and now looked at his eyes. She could tell he was not aware or what was going on.

Glenn said, "Adele Thompson had this set up thinking you would leave me, and tear up my family. She just didn't know you. You've seen enough things to know who I am. I'm going to take these pictures and show them to Charlie and Marvin, and see what they say.

"Oh, Glenn, don't do that. Everyone will know then."

"No they won't Annie, those men are solid. They'll help me get Adele, because they will know, they're next."

"Just so those pictures don't get out."

"Well, prepare yourself. When Adele finds out you are true to me, she'll probably post them all over town. People will know what happened, and won't buy her garbage. She needs to be in jail. I'll bet the warden in Jefferson, fell for her act. She's beautiful, but purely evil."

Glenn packed up the pictures and drove straight to Charlie's house.

Glenn didn't say a word. He just lay down the pictures on their table. Charlie said, "Adele."

Marvin said, "It has to be Adele."

My wife thought the same, boys. We have to find that woman and put her in jail."

Marvin said, "She would have to have lived here to pull this off. Glenn you work on the whores. They will know who set this up, and all the people who helped her."

The next day the three of them found the whores. Glenn said, "Unless you tell me who hired you, and all the people involved, you will go to prison."

The women were scared now. They said, "There were two woman. But the dark headed one, gave the orders. She told us she had a skin disease, and could only watch sex now. We didn't know she would send those pictures to your wife, or we would never have done the job. She and her helper liked to watch. The older one was really into it, but the younger one who had the scarves and dark glasses on, didn't seem that moved.

"Lonnie and Burt are just smalltime crooks who would do anything for another bottle. However, they may know where the women live."

They found Lonnie and Burt, but they couldn't tell them much. They described the woman who hired them, but never got a look at her, because of the glasses and scarves. They described the older lady, but that didn't help much.

Glenn said, "We're back where we started. I would bet she's located in a town close to Santa Fe. It wouldn't be a small town. I think we can rule Albuquerque and Denver out, as too many people could identify her. That leaves Pueblo or Colorado Springs. She's in one of those places.

Glenn said, "We need to have someone in both places. Charlie, she knows you too well. I bet she could identify you without seeing your face. She don't know me that well, and I don't think she knows you that well, Marvin. Why don't' we disguise ourselves and start a surveillance. She probably won't use the same disguise or in the same way, now. However, we have a pretty good description of the other woman. Burt heard her called Karen. Not an unusual name, but not that prevalent either. I bet if we covered the markets, and asked the butchers and store keepers, we could come up with Karen. Then Karen will lead us to Adele.

"If your willing, I will give you a badge as a private detective. Check in with the police before you do anything. Tell them that you believe Adele is living in their city, and that she is an escaped convict doing life in the woman's prison at Jefferson City. I'll have the warrants for her in a couple of days.

"I don't think she is going anyplace, because she still wants Charlie and you, Marvin."

CHAPTER 15

Looking for Adele

B Y THE END of the week, they were on their way. Marvin was in Colorado Springs by the third day. He had worn a gray wig and old clothes. His hat was worn, and his pants old. He dropped by the livery stable and left his horse. He asked the hostler if he knew of a cheap place to live. He pointed to a large house.

He said, "The widow Pavin owns it, and she needs boarders. She is barely getting by. How long do you plan on staying?"

"I don't know. If I can find work, I'll stay awhile."

"What do you do?"

"A little of this and a little of that. What's needed, generally."

"Well, good luck. Tell the widow Pavin I sent you. Her first name is Mary. That may help me, as I plan to court her next year when she's done with her grievin'"

"I'll do that. I'll even tell her you're a right steady feller, if you'll give my horse some oats now and then."

"You've got a deal, Mister."

Marvin changed clothes, and took off his wig. He shaved and combed his hair, and put on a clean shirt. He knew if the widow were to let him a room, he must look clean cut. Mrs. Pavin's boarding house fit his purpose, as it was near the center of town, and he could walk to all the stores.

Mary Pavin was not that old. About thirty-five, if Marvin's estimation of women's ages were correct. She had a wide smile for Marvin. She asked, "How long are you planning to stay Mr. Ellis?"

"It depends. If I can find work, I may be here for some time. By the way, the hostler down at the livery stable sent me. He looks like a steady fellow."

"Oh, that's Otis Taylor. He's been eying me ever since Bill died. He must be twice my age, and just look at him. He always has tobacco juice running into his beard. I ask you, "Would anyone want a man like that."

"I can't answer your question, Ma'am. However, I can surely see why he wants to eye you."

This made Mary blush. She said, "Why Mr. Ellis, you've made me blush. I guess I'm not that old after all."

"You're a quite a lovely woman. You have a pretty face and a young woman's body."

"You keep saying those things, and I'm liable to give you free rent," she laughed.

"I have two rooms available. One is at the back, toward the barn and corrals. The other is upstairs next to Sara Quinn. Once you see her, you'll never look at me again."

"I don't know Mrs. Pavin, you're quite a lady, and beauty is in the eye of the beholder."

"I swear if you keep saying those things I'm going to set my cap for you."

Marvin really laughed as did she. Marvin said, "We really hit it off haven't we. You remind me of woman I met in Gallup, New Mexico. She had a sense of humor like that. I hope we find time to get to know each other."

About that time Sara Quinn walked down the stairs. Mary was right, once you saw Sara you looked no further. She had an hourglass figure and was gorgeous. She gave Marvin a large smile and said, "Mrs. Pavin, you are certainly sprucing up this place." She then extended her hand and said, "I'm Sara Quinn."

Marvin said, "I'm Marvin Ellis. Mrs. Pavin was just telling me how beautiful you were, just before you came down the stairs."

She turned to Mary and said, "Thank you, Mrs. Pavin. That was a nice complement. I could say the same about you."

Marvin said, "I am surrounded by beautiful women. If I had a job, I would try to spark you both."

They both laughed and Mary said, "Watch out Miss Quinn, he possesses a silver tongue. Ten minutes around him and you'll be in his arms."

"Has he been here ten minutes, yet?"

"No, but we'll try to keep him here a long time."

"Where do you hail from, Mr. Ellis?"

For the last few years, Santa Fe. I decided to have a look at Colorado. Colorado Springs looks just like the size and structure I was seeking. It certainly has beautiful women.

"Mrs. Pavin was telling me that she had two rooms available, one next to you and one at the back of the house.

I had better take the one at the back of the house. You and Mrs. Pavin are too much for a dumb cowboy like me. I might forget myself."

Sara said, "Mrs. Pavin, You have outdone yourself with this one. He makes a woman forget herself. I feel I have known him half my life, and it's only been about three or four minutes. Do you feel that way?"

"Yes, he surely has a wonderful spirit about him. I'll bet you're married with seven children, Mr. Ellis."

"No, I'm not married, but I have adopted four children. Two are Mexican and I love them like they were my own. The other two are twins, and I am helping raise them along with my partner, Charlie Thompson."

"Charlie Thompson is your partner! My lord, he owns half of New Mexico. What are you doing staying in boarding house in Colorado Springs, Mr. Ellis."

Marvin knew he had said too much. He said, "May I take you both into my confidence."

They both leaned toward him with serious faces and both said together, "Of course."

"I am here to catch an escaped criminal who is threatening our lives. Please don't say anything about this. It could cost me my life."

Sara said, "Oh, we won't. Can we help you in anyway?"

"Yes, you possibly could. I'll let you know when the time comes. Why don't we start off by changing my name. Let's call me Bill, just plain Bill."

"You are anything but plain, but Bill it is. I like that, don't you, Miss Quinn?"

Marvin said, "Let's drop our Miss and Mrs. now that we're co-conspirators."

"Sounds good to me, unless we are with the other guests," said Mary.

"I will have to change my looks some as the party I am after would know me from afar."

"How do you plan to do that?" asked Sara.

"I have a wig and different clothes to make me look much older."

Marvin needed to pick up his things at the livery stable, so he left them.

Marvin thought to himself, *"I hope respect is always given to older people. It's a charm that nearly all Americans possess."*

Marvin went to the finest hotel in Colorado Springs, and it was just down the street. He asked to see the owner. After being shown into his office, the owner, Carl Henderson, asked, "How may I help you, Mr. Ellis?"

"I'm an undercover detective looking for a person who may be staying in your hotel. This person is a fugitive from the federal prison in Jefferson City, Missouri. I want to sit in your lobby at times, pretending to read a newspaper, so I may apprehend this person, if you will permit me."

"My lord! Is he dangerous?"

"It's not a he, it's a she. She is very beautiful, and can beguile a man very easily with her beauty and charm. However, she is as dangerous as a rattlesnake. She kills without conscious. She has killed before, and swindled many others out of their life's savings."

Henderson was aghast, and his face showed astonishment as he mumbled, "I will permit you to sit in the lobby if you will promise me that no shooting or violence will occur, I must protect my guests, you see."

"That sounds more than reasonable. If she shows up, I will simply follow her out of your building, then have the authorities make the arrest." He then left for the livery stable.

What Marvin didn't realize, was that Adele had spotted him going to the boarding house from the livery stable. She was just coming out of a ladies' store when she saw him. She stepped back in and pretended to be looking at some clothes. When he walked by the ladies' shop, she dropped her head. She waited a minute or so, then came out the door of the shop, and watched as he headed toward Mrs. Pavin's boarding house. She then knew where he would be staying.

Adele had a corner room at the hotel, that had a view of Mrs. Pavin's boarding house. This gave her an opportunity to observe Marvin's comings and goings. She returned to her room in time to see Marvin going back to the livery stable to pick up his saddlebags.

Adele decided to call on the local sheriff. She was a past master at acting. She went and dressed the roll she wanted to play. She entered the sheriff's office. He was alone, as his deputy had just gone to get the prisoners lunch.

She said, "Are you the sheriff?"

Sheriff Anderson rose and said, "Yes I am, Madam. How may I help you?"

"I spotted a man who is very dangerous. He tried to rape me in Denver. He has killed many people. He often disguises himself, so he can work his treachery. I think he is here to rob the bank. He has a gang, but he comes in alone a day ahead of his robbery. His gang then drifts into town the next day. It gives him time to plan the robbery. I would like to assist you in apprehending this man."

The sheriff stood and said, "Where may I find him?"

Adele rolled her eyes at him and said, "My, you are a handsome man. Are you married?"

Sheriff Anderson said, "No, not at the present time."

Adele then walked toward him. She came within a foot of him and said, "I have a corner room at the hotel. He is staying at the boarding house. We can observe him from my window. He is very dangerous and has killed several men who thought they were tough. He carries multiple weapons. One is a derringer up his left sleeve, and he uses it when men are looking at his gun hand. Please let me assist you, I could never forgive myself if you were hurt."

The sheriff was completely captivated by Adele's beauty. He said, "I would love for you to help me. Shall we go to your room?"

As they passed the hotel clerk Sheriff Anderson said, "I'm on official business, Carl. No one is to know that I am using Miss Thompson's room to observe a criminal. I mean no one!" The clerk then dismissed the thought of Adele being the crook Mr. Ellis had told him about.

They proceeded up the stairs to Adele's room. When they arrived, Adele suggested that they move the coach in front of the window. They sat there for awhile and Adele sat close to the sheriff. She leaned against him, as she pretended to crane her neck toward the window. The sheriff was now under her spell. She smelled nicely, and her warm breast was against his chest. She looked up at him and said, "I adore big men who are powerful like you, Sheriff." The sheriff put his arm around her, and she kissed him on the cheek.

As the sheriff moved to fully embrace her she said, "I think I saw him! The sheriff quickly turned his eyes toward the window. Adele took this moment to rise and say, "Would you have a drink, Sheriff, while we wait?"

The sheriff said, "Yes, I would like that." After his drink Adele said, "Why take a chance, why not get your deputy to help you. He could be behind that tree there, and if Mr. Ellis tries anything, your deputy could shoot him before you're in danger."

"That's an excellent idea, Miss Thompson."

"Please call me, Adele, now that we are so intimate."

"Okay, Adele. I will go get my deputy."

While the sheriff was gone, Adele asked the hotel clerk if he had someone to take a message. He said he did, and called to a boy who was sweeping up.

Adele said, "Tell the boardinghouse owner that the hotel wants to see her new roomer about a letter sent to him."

The boy took off and Adele waited at the door of the hotel. She saw the deputy getting into position, and the sheriff was instructing him. The boy started back, and shortly Marvin came out of the boarding house. Adele stepped quickly toward him. Marvin saw her as she approached. He came toward her and as he did, she tore her dress so that her breasts fell out as Marvin approached her.

The Sheriff yelled, "Don't make a move! My deputy and I have our guns trained on you. One small move by you, and we'll shoot."

Marvin said, "As you can see, I'm unarmed. This woman is an escaped convict from Jefferson Federal Women's Prison."

The sheriff said, "Tom, if a derringer appears in his hand, shoot him dead." Upon stating this, the sheriff approached Marvin with his gun cocked. Adele still had her breasts showing, and made no attempt to hide them."

The sheriff cuffed Marvin hands behind his back. He then searched him and found no weapons.

Adele said, "I formally charge this man with attempted rape."

The sheriff looked at her beautiful breasts and said, "Duly charged, Madam."

Marvin was taken to jail. He knew that nothing he could say would be heard by the sheriff, as he saw the glint in his eye. Tom, the deputy, was mesmerized, also. Adele then stuffed her breasts back into her dress.

When they reached the jail, Sheriff Anderson said, "I need to attend Miss Thompson, Tom. She is really fragile, and I must soothe her. Be very cautious with that prisoner. He has brought down several lawmen in the past."

Sheriff Anderson then left and went to the hotel. Adele was there with a bottle of brandy. She poured him three fingers in a water glass. She had poured herself some tea that looked like the brandy.

While they sipped their drinks, Adele said, "Would you help me pin my dress?"

The sheriff moved over, and Adele moved his hands until they were touching her breasts and said, "Hold it right there, Sheriff, while I put in the pin."

Adele then said, "I guess I should reward you for being so

brave, and keeping that beast off me." She then took him in her arms and gave him a passionate kiss."

By this time the sheriff was in love. He had never been with a woman of Adele's beauty and charm.

Adele then said, "Please excuse me Sheriff, but I must bathe and change clothes."

As the sheriff was leaving she said, "Please don't listen to that man, Sheriff. He will tell all kind of lies to save himself. You and your deputy are witnesses to his attempted rape."

While Sheriff Anderson was gone. Mavin said, "Deputy, I will give you ten dollars to wire the Jefferson Federal Prison in Jefferson, Missouri. Here is twenty dollars. That woman is Adele Thompson, an escaped prisoner who was serving a life sentence for murdering my wife. Didn't you see her rip her own dress before I was five feet from her?"

Tom thought and said, "Yes. It appeared that way to me. I'll send your wire." He left and went to the telegraph office and sent the wire. He asked that the return wire be sent to Sheriff Anderson with a copy to him.

As the sheriff had spent much time in Adele's room, Tom returned before the sheriff. Tom decided to say nothing, as he could see that the sheriff was completely enamored with Adele. He knew that nothing but hard facts would convince the sheriff, and maybe not even then.

The sheriff brought the charge of attempted rape against Marvin, and took his arrest charges to Judge Putnam. The judge set the arraignment for the next day at nine o'clock. Sheriff Anderson went to Adele's hotel room, but she had checked out. The hotel manager said, "She left a note for you."

The sheriff opened the envelope and it read:

"Dear Sheriff Anderson,

The trauma of this was too much for me. I also was falling in love with you. Please forgive me as I am so frightened, I must leave. I will keep you close to my heart. Don't let that man lie to you. Beat him if he does. He deserves something for trying to rape me.

With my deepest love,
Adele."

As the Sheriff came to the courtroom a telegram was delivered to him. It read:

THE WOMAN, ADELE THOMPSON, IS AN ESCAPED CONVICT STOP APPREHEND HER AS SOON AS POSSIBLE STOP WARDEN AVERY JOHNSON, JEFFERSON FEDERAL PRISON STOP

The sheriff was so irritated that he just wadded up the telegram, and threw it into the trash. Tom, his deputy, saw him do this, and as the sheriff walked into the courtroom, Tom reached into the trash and pulled out the wire.

Judge Putman had his clerk read the indictment to the court. He then called the sheriff to testify. Sheriff Anderson told how Marvin Ellis had ripped Adele Thompson's dress exposing her breasts, and that he and his deputy, Tom Perkins, had arrested him.

Judge Putman turned to Tom Perkins and said, "Does

Sheriff Anderson's description of the crime fit what you saw, Deputy Perkins?"

"No, your honor, it doesn't. He was then sworn in, much to Sheriff Anderson's chagrin. The Judge then asked Tom to describe what he saw.

Tom said, "As Mr. Ellis approached Miss Thompson, she ripped her own dress and cried, 'Rape! He is trying to rape me!' Mr. Ellis had not touched her."

The judge was appalled and said, "Is Deputy Perkin's statement true, Sheriff? Remember, you are still under oath, and one of you could be charged with perjury."

The sheriff then saw he was in a bind. He loved Adele, but could now see how she used him. He reluctantly said, "Deputy Perkin's statement is true now that I remember the incident. It all happened so fast that I thought the man was trying to rape the woman when she yelled."

The judge said, "Let the record show that both the sheriff, and his deputy, say that the woman ripped her own dress, and tried to make it look like a rape."

The deputy then took out the wadded telegram and said, "I would also like to enter this telegram into evidence. The sheriff then realized the deputy had the telegram he had wadded up.

The judge read the telegram and Tom said, "I received this telegram and was going to give it to the sheriff, but he was already in the courtroom."

The judge said, "I see you have the wrong person in custody, Sheriff. Where is Miss Thompson?"

The sheriff said, "She left on the morning train, your honor. I see she played me for a fool, and I fell for it."

The judge smiled and said, "We've all been there, Sheriff. Release the prisoner."

Marvin went back to the rooming house, and told Mary that the fugitive had left town, and he must follow her.

Mary returned his money and said, "You never spent a night here, so I can't charge you. You're leaving two broken hearted girls, but remember, you now have women in the port of Colorado Springs."

Marvin said, "I want to tell you, I have seldom met two lovelier women, and I am sad to leave you. I just wonder had I stayed, if romance would have developed."

"There he goes again, Sara. In another day or two I would be in love, so it's a good thing he's leaving."

Sara said, "I feel the same way. You have charmed us until we are not ourselves. Just think what might have happened, Mary."

"I am trying my best to imagine that, Sara," and they all laughed as Marvin took his leave.

Marvin took the train to Pueblo, where he knew Glenn would be. As he traveled he thought of the two women. They were both a delight, and he thought of what Mary had said, *"What might have developed if he had stayed."*

CHAPTER 16

A Day of Reconning

IN PUEBLO, MARVIN went to the best hotel in town and asked if a Glenn Truan was registered there. The clerk looked at the register and said, "No, there's no one under that name here.

Marvin said, "Let me see the register, and showed his badge. The clerk turned the register around and Marvin looked down the list of names. He saw Max Truman that looked like Glenn's handwriting.

Marvin asked, "What room is Max Truman in?"

"201 at the head of the stairs, Sir."

Marvin went up the stairs and knocked on 201. Glenn was surprised to see Marvin.

He said, "How did you find me?"

Marvin grinned and said, "I'm a detective, remember?" This brought a smile to Glenn's face and he said, I'll get my coat."

Marvin said, "No, pack your bag. Adele escaped from me, and is headed toward Albuquerque. She's a day ahead of us. I'll tell you about it on the train."

As they were traveling, Marvin told him the story. Then asked, "Where could she be heading?"

Glenn said, "I don't think she will stop in Albuquerque, unless she plans on taking a stage to throw us off. She now knows we're after her, and may be feeling the heat. With two of us, she can't pull much with both of us watching each other's back. However, she doesn't know there are two of us, so that will help. What do you think she might do?"

"I think she's heading for El Paso. She knows she's a day ahead of me, but knows I will be following her. I think she will go to El Paso, and that a new railroad has been built that goes from El Paso to Houston. From there she could catch a ship around the coast to Virginia. She always returns there, because she's a native."

Glenn said, "Funny, I just finished reading a new book by Thomas Hardy, *Return of the Native.* He says you can never go back, because everything changes."

"You'll have to loan it to me when we return."

They both sat awhile not talking, then Marvin said, "How could we beat her to Virginia.?"

"That's easy, we could board a train in El Paso that goes to Kansas City. Then catch another train to St. Louis. I know they have a railroad that goes from there to Richmond. If she takes a ship to Virginia, It goes much slower than the train, so we ought to make up the day we're behind.

"Most of the ships that go up Chesapeake Bay, go to the port at Virginia Beach. We could go to the harbormaster and ask him about ships from Miami, and meet the ships when they dock."

"Well, I'm willing if you are, and I will foot the bill of our travel."

"I'm glad you said that, because I'm about tapped out."

"I'm not saying this to brag, Glenn, but Charlie and I have accumulated great wealth in the past ten years. Charlie made the money, but years ago we became partners, and all our wealth is in both our names, as we are closer than brother."

"I'm not wealthy at all, but I enjoy my job and it's a living."

They arrived at Virginia Beach just four days later, and went directly to the harbormaster. He gave them the schedule of all ships coming from Miami.

They stayed at a hotel near the docking area, then met the first ship. She was not aboard. The next ship came the next day, and she was not on that ship either. There was a ship that night that docked at two a. m. No one got off the ship as they were all in their cabins sleeping.

Marvin went aboard and met the captain. Glenn showed his badge and the warrants, then described Adele to him.

A smile crossed his face and he said, "I'm nearly sure you have described Dora Thompson. She's in cabin 37 on the main deck. I imagine she's asleep, as we advised them all to stay aboard and get a good night's sleep."

Glenn said, "Good, that will give us time to get the police here to make the arrest."

They went to the police station and Glenn produced the warrant for Adele. Captain Dials came with them. It was now turning morning. The ship captain knocked on her hatch and said, "Mrs. Thompson! She opened the hatch in her robe sleepy-eyed and said, "What's the matter, Captain."

Glenn, Marvin and Captain Dial were standing behind

the hatch, so that she couldn't see them. The captain said, "There's an emergency, and you must get dressed and leave the ship."

She closed the hatch, and about ten minutes later appeared with her suitcase. She came out, and saw the police captain, Marvin and Glenn. She thought about running, but knew that would do no good, so she just came along meekly.

Although it took two weeks to get her back to the prison in Jefferson, Glenn and Marvin waited and accompanied the officers who took her back. They both wanted to be sure she was back in prison.

Marvin had wired the warden, and he and Alma met them at the gate of the prison.

Avery had a large smile on his face as did Alma.

Avery said, "Welcome back, Adele. Everyone has missed you. We know you will be happy. We have a special cellmate for you."

There was no interview, She was given a shower, and put into her prison suit and taken directly to a cell.

Adele saw a very large woman and Alma said, Norma, this is your new cellmate, Adele Thompson.

Norma said, "I've waited a long time for you, Baby, I'm glad you're finally here."

The cell door closed and Avery and Alma walked away smiling.

Norma said, "I have a treat for you tonight, Adele. I do favors for the night guards and they get me things I want. Tonight around midnight, you will take down your pants, and put your bare butt to the bars. I'll hold you tight to the bars You're going to be very popular with the guards, I promise."

Adele was aghast. She said, "What can I do to get out of this?"

"Nothing, Honey, you're mine, now. I own you. However, if you perform well, and give me great pleasure, I will spare you from servicing the guards at night. Just remember, I need a lot of loving. I do like a change of girls ever so often, and I might trade you for some fresh, new girl. I can get this done through Alma.

"I do things for Alma, because she treats me right. She can change cell assignments. She likes young girls, and won't want you. I'm the opposite, I like women who have experience. You probably have no experience with women, but you are pretty enough, so I'll train you. If you learn fast and show enthusiasm, I may begin to like you."

Adele knew she was in for a bad time, and the only way out of it was to please Norma. She thought, *"There is another way, if I killed Norma, but how. If I killed Norma, what more could they do to me? Maybe hang me. Hanging would be better than living a life pleasing Norma. I can bear anything for awhile. It will just take planning. I may be able to get a knife from the mess hall. It will need a sharp point so I can put it through Norma's neck while making love to her. I must be accurate and not miss the main artery. She may still be able to kill me before she bleads to death, but that's a chance I must take."* Adele was able to smuggle a knife out of the mess hall. She hid it in the yard and sharpened it everyday in the yard. No one came around her. They all knew she was Norma's girl, and no one fooled with Norma.

In three weeks time she had the knife to a fine point by rubbing it against the concrete of a corner of the wall. She also used a hard rock she had found. Meanwhile her life in the cell with Norma was tolerable. After the second week, she didn't have to service the guards at night, which inerupted her sleep.

She acted like she was falling in love with Norma. She would give her passionate kisses and used her mouth around Norma's neck and ears. Norma loved this, as no other woman ever did that. Adele would kiss her around her ears until Norma breathed deeply, and was wild with desire.

Several times Adele would whisper, I love you, Norma. Norma had never had a woman say that to her. Adele's love began to make Norma tender toward her, and when Adele would say, "I love you, Norma," Norma would whisper, "I love you, too."

Adele then knew she had her. She would maneuver Norma in this one position where she was kissing her around the ears and neck. Norma would be on her back with her eyes closed. Adele practice reaching her hand under the mattress where she planned to hide her knife. Adele would then push her head to one side opening up her throat. Adele would kiss the neck exactly where she planned to put the knife. She could feel Norma's pulse with her lips.

It had been eight weeks now, and Adele knew she would act that night. She had smuggled the knife into their cell, and hid it under the mattress right where her hand could clutch it easily. When the lights went out, Adele took off her uniform and folded it up on the upper bunk. She laid nude on top of Norma giving her a passionate kiss.

She began kissing Norma around the neck and ears, and

Norma was loving it with her eyes closed. She pushed Norma's head to one side as she had done may times. She kissed her neck finding the exact place to put the knife. Adele's hand went around the handle of the knife, and she shoved the knife deep into Norma's neck. Blood spurted in a large stream when Adele removed the knife. She had hit the main artery dead center.

Norma was so confused that she hardly felt the knife go in, but she did feel the hot blood squirting out. She tried to get up, but Adele pushed her back down on the bed.

Adele said, "You were just out of your class, Norma."

She waited until Norma fell limp and the blood quit pulsating. She put blood on Norma's hand and lay the knife down on the floor, as if Norma had dropped it. She went to the sink, and cleaned herself thoroughly. She donned her uniform again, then yelled for the guard. He brought a lantern and saw all the blood. He blew his whistle, and all the guards came to the cell. Adele just backed into a corner.

They tried to revive Norma as her body was warm. It was ten minutes before Alma came. Alma took her lantern up to Adele's face and said, "What happened?"

Adele said, "I really don't know. Norma yelled, and I came off the top bunk and saw she had killed herself. She had told me she was in love with me, just before we went to bed, but I told her I could never love her. She was madley in love with me, and I think that's why she committed suicide."

At the inquest Adele stuck to her story. As Norma was so much larger and stronger than Adele, they all believed her story. They saw no way that Adele could overpower a person as big and strong as Norma.

The guard that first saw Norma, testified that Norma may have still been alive, and that they did everything possible to revive her. He also said, "Adele had no blood on her, which would be impossible if she had put the knife in Norma."

Adele said, "How could I get a knife. I've just been here a little over eight weeks and Norma would not let the other women near me in the yard. I could never cut anyone with a knife, much less stab someone. I'm so sorry for Norma. If I had known she would do something like that, I would have never told her I could never love her." By this time Adele was weeping.

The inquiry board unanimously exonerated Adele. Alma put her in another cell with another large woman. When they were alone, Adele said, "I own you. If you get out of line, just remember what happened to Norma.

The woman's name was Hester. She realized that Adele was in for murder, and became frightened. Adele said in a surly voice, "Get me a cup of water, I'm thirsty."

Hester immediately got up, and fetched her a cup of water. Adele then said, "If you will do everything I tell you, we can own this prison. We must form a gang. Eventually, we may be able to escape from this hellhole. Are you with me."

Hester said, "Yes Ma'am." Adele then knew she had her. The guards took a new atitude toward Adele, as most believed she had killed Norma. None believe Norma would take her own life.

Slowly Adele brought women into her gang. She made them promise on their life, that they would be loyal to her. She began holding meetings in the courtyard. She now had over twenty women who were true to her. She selected who she wanted in her gang, and nearly everyone wanted in.

Even though she was dressed in prison garb with no makeup, she was still a beauty. She noticed one of the women prison guards eying her some. The guard had been promoted to be the supervisor of the courtyard recently. Her name was Polly Turner.

Adele called her over by having one of her women tell the supervisor that she wanted to see her. She dismissed the other women and said, "I need to talk to this screw, alone." They left as Polly came over. She said, "You wanted to see me?"

"Yes. I'll be as brief as I can. I'm a wealthy woman. I have over a fifty thousand dollars in a bank in Virginia. I have a fool proof way to escape with very little risk to you. I will give you ten thousand dollars to help me. As I said, it will be very little risk on your part, but escential to me.

"I need you to open a post office box in Jefferson under the name of Dora Thomson. I will then give you a letter to smuggle out and mail. The letter will be to my Virginia bank, asking for an accounting of my savings with them.

"When they send the accounting, you will know that I have the money and can pay you the ten grand. I know a man who delievers groceries to the prison. They search the wagons thoroughly, but my friend has a space to put me in that cannot be found.

"I will need you to contact this man. His name is Paco. Offer Paco a hundred dollars to smuggle me out. He did it once before. No one could ever figure out how I escaped once before, but Alma. She helped once before with this same scheme. We must wait for a time that she is on vacation. You can find that out. Then we can start our planning. Are you interested?"

"Of course. Ten thousand dollars is enough for me to retire and get out of this hellhole. Give me the letter to your bank tomorrow when you're in the yard. I know who Paco is. He smiles at me a lot. He probably wants to get in my pants. I will visit him at his home."

The next day Adele gave the letter to Polly. Polly had checked the vacation schedule, and to their delight, Alma was slated to go for a two weeks vacation the next month. Polly mailed the letter and a couple of weeks later the Virginia bank sent the accounting.

Polly then met with Adele and said, "I got the letter from your bank, and see you can pay me. Alma takes her vacation in four weeks. I talked to her, and she said she was going to New Orleans, so we're nearly set."

Adele said, "After I'm in Paco's wagon he will leave and follow the other wagons. After a half mile, and out of sight of the prison, Paco will stop. You will be there with a buggy to pick me up. Have a tarp that I can hide under. We will travel to a farm just north of the prison about five miles on the Dixon road. There is an enormous oak tree beside the lane leading into the farm. You can't miss it. The farm was vacant the last time I was there, but it could be occupied now. Go to that farm, and if it is occupied, tell them you need to rent their barn for a month as you are buying some horses. Offer them twenty dollars. I'm sure they will go for that.

"There's a hidden room in the barn. I will tell you how to access it. Then you must stock the room with food for me as

I will stay there a week. The authorities will look for me that long, then they'll give up.

"I'll need jars of fruit, vegetables and beef jerky to last me that week. Also bring bed clothing. I will stay there one week, then you will come with a buggy dressed as a man. You will bring clothes for me that older women wear. I will need a scarf and dark glasses, also. Bring a tarp for me to hide under, until we are clear of the farm.

"We will then go into Jefferson and make the transaction. I will order the transfer of money and write you a check for ten thousand after the money arrives. Do you have any place I can stay while we're waiting for the money?"

"Yes, my mother left me a house. It sits at the edge of town. If we come late at night, no one will know you're there. I will go back to the prison, and no one will know the difference. It will take a week or more for the money to arrive. You'll be alright at my house. I have stocked a lot of groceries there. No one ever comes to see me, as they know I work at the prison and stay there at night.

Everything went like Adele planned it. Paco came and no one saw Adele get into the space Paco had, and they were off. Polly took her to the barn and she stayed for a week. Polly then came and drove her to her house. Polly left her there and returned to the prison. During the time they waited for the transfer of money, Adele made arrangements for her travel.

A week later Polly returned and took Adele to the bank. They made the transaction.

Adele didn't try to scam Polly, as she had Alma. She liked her, and suggested that she stay on with the prison for a few months before she resigned.

Adele was now free again. Avery was again stumped on how Adele could escape. Alma was on vacation in New Orleans, and had even sent Avery a card from there. He knew Adele had to have assistance. He suspected a male guard, who he had seen eying Adele. He knew Adele was a master at manipulating men. However, the guard never made contact with Adele, so he could see no way he could smuggle Adele out. There were just too many guards. If more than one were involved then, someone would talk. It was a mystery.

Avery decided he had better write, Charlie and Marvin to let them know that Adele was on the loose again.

CHAPTER 17

The Girls

CHARLIE RECEIVED THE letter and showed it to Marvin. Marvin said, "I think Avery is helping her. How else could she escape that prison?"

Charlie said, "That sounds logical, but why. If he is romantically inclined to her, why would he let her out when he could have her anytime he wants in the prison?"

"She can manipulate men very easily with her beauty and charm. I ought to know. She used me like a dishrag. I can surely see how she can manipulate a man. Do you think we are in any danger?"

"Some I suppose. She will really want to exact revenge on Glenn and me. You, not so much. I think she does love you, Charlie, but she loves herself far more. I think she will lay low for a few years. I would bet she has money stashed away, and if she doesn't, some poor love-starved man will furnish it to her."

"Where do you think she'll go? She's used up a lot of cities in America."

"I would say Europe or Mexico. She speaks no foreign

language, so she might try London. I'll talk to Glenn and see what he thinks."

Glenn agreed. He said, "London's a good guess. Do you want to go over there and see what we find?"

"That may be worth it. Let's talk it over with Charlie."

Charlie said, "No. I think you would waste your time. She's been to Mexico and knows her way around. She may even have picked up some of their lingo as she was there a long time, according to the warden. That told me he was involved with her. Like I said, she can charm a monkey out of a tree.

"I will say one thing, it does no good to put her in prison. I suggest the grave the next time she's caught." This shocked both Glenn and Marvin, but after they thought about how many lives she had ruined, they both agreed, although not stating it.

***

The girls were home for the summer. They both hugged and kissed Charlie and Marvin. Lydia had Marvin and Lisa, Charlie. The boys worked them hard, but also wined and dined them most nights. People saw them, and how the girls hung onto them. This caused a lot of talk as the girls were now fully women, and showed every inch of it.

The minister of their church called on Charlie and Marvin, and said, "Brothers, some women of the church came to me and asked me to speak to you about your two girls."

"What do you want to know, parson?" Charlie asked.

"It's a touchy subject, you know."

"Your women want to know if we are sleeping with the girls, don't they, Parson?"

"The parson squirmed in his chair, and turn red then said, "Something like that I suppose."

"Call a meeting of the women who asked you to come here to be there. We would like to fully address that question. Don't tell them we'll be there. This will take you off the hook, and we can probably satisfy their curiosity."

The parson agreed, and the meeting was held in the auditorium of the church. The women were aghast when both Charlie and Marvin came in.

Charlie said, "The parson came to us and said you ladies wanted to know if we were sleeping with our daughters. So, we decided to address that question to you, but first I would like to know how many of you had sex before you were married. Just raise your hands if you did."

The women were so stunned, and sat in utter shock. Charlie then said, "Now you see how inappropriate you were in asking us such a question. In church Sunday, I will name each one of you, and tell the congregation what you asked us. Do you want me to tell them about the question I asked you?"

The women began filling out and the parson said, "You came down hard on them, Charlie."

"You are not so innocent yourself, parson. You should have addressed that question yourself, and never involved us. We're quite disappointed in you. We'll see you Sunday."

After they were out of the church, Marvin said, "I'll bet none of those women are in church Sunday. Well, they have to come back sometime, and they know we'll be there waiting."

Most of the women told their husbands about the meeting.

To a man the men said, "You stuck your nose into something that you had no business doing. You're going to church Sunday, if I have to drag you. You have to take your medicine. I know Charlie and Marvin will be there every week, so you might as well face the music now."

Mrs. Bowers said, "I'll address the congregation before Charlie does. I will tell them what we did, and how inappropriate it was. I will then turn to Marvin and Charlie and apologize for our questioning their integrity. If I know Charlie, he will be gracious."

Sunday came and before the parson opened with the morning prayer, Mrs. Bowers stood and said, "Myself and several of the women of the church questioned Charlie's and Marvin's integrity about their daughters. My dear husband," and she turned to him with tears in her eyes, "Set me straight. I sincerely apologize for our action. Mr. Thomson and Mr. Ellis, you are pillars of this church and God's family. I'm sure the rest of the women involved agree with me."

Charlie stood and said, "Marvin and I do have two lovely daughters that love us dearly as we do them. I don't know how any of this came to this point, but now that it has come to light, let's put it to bed. We will continue to love our daughters and they us.

"As you know, they have finished two years of schooling back East and have an other year to complete it. We will then assess the issue at that time."

He sat down then Mr. Bowers stood and started clapping, the others stood until the whole auditorium was clapping.

Marvin and Charlie just smiled and nodded.

After church Lydia said, "I didn't fully understand what that was all about, Marvin. Could you enlighten us?"

Marvin said, "Some women of the church wanted to know if we were sleeping with you, so we thought we would address that this morning,. However, Mrs. Bowers preempted us with an apology."

Lisa said, "They should have asked me. I would have said, "To my disappointment, Charlie won't sleep with me, but if he did, I would be thrilled."

Charlie said, "Praise God, she didn't understand, Marvin. They may have stoned us."

Lydia said, "When a woman loves someone, like we do, she should love him with all her mind and body and someday we will have that pleasure, Lisa."

Marvin and Charlie just shook their heads in silence. Both were thinking it's only two more weeks until they go back.

***

Adele had decided that she would go to Guadalajara. She thought this city large enough to provide her with the comforts she required, and still be an unlikely place for anyone to look for her. When she arrived, she stayed in a nice hotel. She was talking to a couple who had just retired. They told her of a place some forty miles south, where many Americans and Canadians were living.

She caught the stage and was elated with what she found. There were over a thousand Americans and Canadians in the area. She found she could not buy a house, so she rented one. She interviewed several maids, and picked one who spoke some English. She told her that one of her duties was to teach her Spanish. The lessons began the first day.

It took only a week until everyone knew the beautiful Adele, now with the last name of Winters. She had picked that name as it was now winter in America.

She met a couple in their late thirties that she liked. His name was Thad Rice and her name was Leah. The man was handsome and the woman shapely. They were at a dance one night and it was not uncommon for women to dance with other women at times. One of the other women had pulled Thad up, as she wanted to dance with him. So Adele said, "Let's dance, Leah."

As they were dancing, Leah said, "Tell me something about yourself, Adele." Adele said, "I was married to a man named Charlie Thompson in Santa Fe. I just grew tired of him. He's a nice upstanding man, but boring. I want an exciting life and he was a drag on me.

"I couldn't have that life in Santa Fe, as we went to church every Sunday. We went to parties where everyone there was sixty years old or older. I guess I'm over sexed, but I desire younger men, and to be with younger people, such as you and Thad.

"I like it here. The people we see are young and vibrant. I don't think I will marry again, because marriage ties you down too much."

"Wow, you are a wild one. I can see your point. However, I love Thad and would be lost without him."

What Leah didn't know was that Adele liked Thad, too. She thought that sooner or later she would find a way to be with him.

They had drinks together several nights, and often dined together. One night Thad told how they lived in Chicago where he worked for a gang. He said, "I was a bag man for them. The gang did a lot of illegal things, but their main trade was bootlegging liquor from Canada.

"Then this man came to Chicago. His name was Bill Buchannan. He took over the town, and told our boss if he wanted to stay healthy, he would find a new place to live.

"I was leaving for Canada with twenty grand to buy more booze. I knew our time in Chicago was over so I told Leah we were leaving.

"Instead of Canada we came here. I had read about this place in a magazine some months before we came. We had enough cash to last us for life, so we left and haven't regretted a day of it."

Adele liked to be with them, but wanted Thad. She never showed it though.

One day Leah received a letter from her sister. She told how their mother was very low, and she needed to come.

They talked it over and Leah said, "I must go. No one much knew me, so I know it will be safe."

Thad said, "No matter, take my colt. Keep it in your purse, and keep your purse close."

Leah said, "Adele, you keep care of Thad for me. I shouldn't be over two weeks, but don't get anxious if it's longer."

Adele waited a couple of nights after Leah left, then invited Thad over. They had dinner and then some drinks. Adele could see that she would have to play it slow as she knew Thad loved Leah very much.

She waited another few days then invited him again. This

time she said, "I decided I would take you to a restaurant, and buy you a dinner."

Thad said, "I really ought to pay as you fixed me dinner the other day."

The restaurant had a band and a dance floor. Adele got him to dance with her, and she danced very close. Thad didn't pull away, so she worked her charm on him. When they were walking home, Adele suggested that they have a drink at her house before he went home. The one drink turned into several.

As Thad was leaving Adele came into his arms, and it was easy to get him into her bedroom. When he was going home he thought, *"That must never happen again. I will refuse to go with her the next time."*

However, just a few nights later, Adele came over and again got him to sleep with her.

***

When Leah arrived she found that her mother had already passed away, and they were having the funeral that day. She just had time to change into her black dress and attend the funeral with her sister and her husband, Ralph.

After the funeral they went to her sister's home. Ralph said, "I don't want to scare you, but they are still looking for Thad. They may know who you are, so if I were you I would get out of town tonight."

Leah heeded his warning and bought a train ticket that night. As she sat in the train station she clutched the revolver in her purse. She was scared, but she braved it and was soon on a train heading south.

Thad had taught her how to use the gun, as he knew the gang he was in were evil. He had told her about some atrocities against disloyal gang members, and their families he had witnessed. So when they had the time, he taught Leah how to use a pistol. She didn't think she would ever have to use it, but she wanted to be able to if she did.

Her trip went well. She marveled that she had been gone only eight days. She decided to surprise Thad. She would slip in the back door and then say, "I'm home."

When she arrived she slipped in the backdoor and could hear some racket coming from the bedroom. The door was open and she could see Thad on top of Adele. They were both nude.

Leah set her purse down and removed the pistol. She slipped in beside Adele with them unaware as they both had their eyes closed. She put the pistol against Adele's temple and pulled the trigger. It killed Adele instantly.

Thad was mortified and scared. He thought she might kill him, also. However Leah in a calm voice said, "Get dressed. We need to get her dressed and put her in a chair in our living room."

Thad was quick to dress and did everything Leah said. They now had Adele dressed and in a chair in their living room. Leah wiped the gun clean, then put it in Adele's hand and closed it on the pistol. She then dropped it on the floor. Little blood showed as the bullet didn't emerge from her head.

Leah said, "Go get a police officer. Tell him there has been a terrible accident. Don't talk to them just come back, and let me do all the talking."

It happened that not far from them he saw a policeman, and waved for him to come, which he did.

When they came into the house, Leah was sitting on another chair and said, "We were taking, and Adele told us she was sick of life. Her husband and she had parted. She said she had nothing left to live for. She then pulled a gun from her purse and shot herself. We were horrified."

The policeman left, and told them not to touch anything. After he left, Leah went and retrieved a bottle of brandy and poured Thad four fingers. She said, "Sip that and when the police arrive, let me do all the talking. Just nod at them, and I will say you are too shocked to talk."

It went down just like Leah wanted. After the police were through, the head detective said, "I'm sorry you had to witness such a thing. Were you close friends?"

"Very close. Have the body sent to the mortuary and we will pay the mortician."

Leah never mentioned Thad's tryst with Adele again. Thad made a mental note that he would never fool around again. The next time it could be him.

Leah paid the mortician to embalm Adele, and send the body to Charlie Thompson in Santa Fe, New Mexico, which he did.

***

A messenger from the depot came to Charlie's office and told him that a coffin had been sent from Mexico to him.

Marvin and Charlie went down to the station. They opened the casket and there lay Adele with a note pinned to her dress. The mortician had fixed her wound so that it wasn't noticeable.

Charlie just stood there and began to cry. Marvin

took him in his arms and said, "She looks so peaceful and beautiful." He took the note and shut the coffin. They went to the undertaker and made arrangements for a graveside service. Word of mouth quickly circulated about Adele, and her graveside service.

Several people came who had known her. Some just out of curiosity. Robert Hargrove was there, and Marvin noticed tears running down his face. Charlie talked and said, "I guess I always loved Adele. She was my only wife and although she did some terrible things, that included killing Marvin's wife, Gloria, it's still hard for me." He turned to Marvin and said, "This wonderful man suffered the most by her hand. The Lord will be Adele's judge."

They closed the grave and walked back to their office. Marvin then remembered the note and pulled it from his pocket and handed it to Charlie. It read,

"Mr. Thompson,

Adele took her own life. I suppose all the things she did came to haunt her, and she could not live with them anymore. We're sorry,

Leah and Thad Rice."

Marvin wrote the warden at the Jefferson Prison and sent the note he had received from Thelma and Thad Rice.

Avery shared the note with Alma. Alma thought, *"Let's see her escape from the devil's prison."*

CHAPTER 18

Graduation and More

IT WAS SPRING again and Charlie and Marvin were traveling to the girl's graduation. As they rode the train, Charlie said, "How are we going to handle the girls?"

"I suppose if they want us to marry them, we'll have to. We promised after they graduated, we would marry them. I can't think of anyone in the world who I had rather be with. I feel their love for me when I'm close to them.

"You said them. Do you love both of them?"

"I suppose I do. How about you, Charlie?"

"Yes, I suppose I love them both. However, Lisa wants me and Lydia wants you."

"Yes, they had to make a decision, but I think had it been that Lydia wanted you and Lisa wanted me, it would be about the same. To me they're nearly the same person."

Charlie said, "We can tell them apart now, but just barely."

"Even their minds think the same way, Charlie. I think that's more remarkable than looking identical. I suppose I'm in love with them. I don't think Gloria would condone our marriages, though."

"I think she would. She would much rather Lydia have you than an other woman. Yes. I think she would condone the marriage. I wonder what the citizens of Santa Fe will have to say."

"I guess we'll have to find out. You can give a speech in church telling them that we had promised the girls if they would graduate from college after three years there, we would marry them. Say, it was in jest at first, but then we came to love them like they did us. Tell them that the girls wore white, legitimately. There will be a few that say, "I told you so, but we can live with that."

They were at the graduation hall and both were wearing white dresses. They looked radiant.

Charlie said, "You look like angels. I've never see a prettier sight."

Marvin said, "Let me see your diplomas, I want to make sure."

Lisa sad, "You know us pretty well, don't you, Marvin."

Marvin looked at both diplomas, then handed them to Charlie.

He nodded and looked at Lisa and said, "Are you holding us to the promise of marrying you?"

"Of course," said Lydia and took Marvin's arm. Why do you think we wore white dresses to the graduation. Let's go get the licenses. We have already arranged for a preacher."

Charlie looked at Marvin and said, "I guess we're hooked."

The girls both grabbed them and kissed them with passion.

They were married that very day. They decided to take a honeymoon aboard a luxury liner. They left from the New

York City harbor. They would go to London, Paris, Rome and then decide from there, where they would go.

They bought the girls anything they wanted. Lisa said, "The first day we saw you, we both agreed, that if mother died, we would marry you. Later Charlie came along and saved us from being bigamists. If you remember, we were six and you were twenty-three. Seventeen years isn't that far apart."

Charlie said, "Twenty-five years is, though."

Lisa said, "You two look the same age."

Marvin said, "You're just like Patti, she decided when she was ten to marry me."

Lydia said, "We were only six, so we saw the opportunity much quicker."

Marvin said, "Well, you got what you wanted, I hope we will never disappoint you. What do you want the most, Lydia?"

"A baby. I want us to each have five babies, if we can."

"Lisa said, "Five is enough. We will move to the Cordova's hacienda and throw a party to end all parties. I want all the crew there with their wives to help us celebrate. I just wish Juanita could have been here as our bride's maid. She's our mother, now. Patti was too young to be our mother. I hope I can love you as much as Patti did, Marvin."

"I think you do. I can still see her at age ten. She loved me like you do."

They were gone four months, and it was fall before they returned. Marvin wanted to be there for the roundup. Lydia then learned she was pregnant.

They were home and both couples were now living at

the Cordova place. They had two maids and had employed a butler who saw to the running of the manor. His name was Eric Mathers. He was from England. He had lost his wife and decided he wanted to leave England. He had seen advertisements about Santa Fe and went there.

He had put an ad in the paper and Charlie saw it. After interviewing him with the girls, he was hired. The girls loved his British accent. He knew just how to run a large place. He reviewed the menus, kept the books, ordered everything that was necessary and made sure they weren't overcharged. He tried to mold the Mexican maids like the ones in England, but there he failed. The maids spoke English well, but they had none of the grace that the English maids had. They just smiled at him when he gave them lectures.

He went to Lydia about them. Lydia said, "There's just somethings you can't change, Eric."

Eric had never been called by his first name in England, and it took him awhile to adjust to the Americans and Mexicans. Although in his fifties, the maids still flirted with him shamelessly, and he could not stop it, so he finally gave up and just smiled back at them.

The cowboys of Charlie's and Marvin's never bothered to knock, they just came in and generally made themselves at home as they had always done. Tim was making a sandwich in the kitchen and Eric walked in and was appalled.

Tim recognized how perturbed Eric was and said, "Sit down Eric. I have a story to tell you. Eric sat down and Tim said, "We have lived with Marvin and Charlie. We fought together and rode thousands of miles together. We are just one big family. Marvin got us to be that way. They don't pay us wages, we have shares in the herd. We are more like partners than cowhands. I know they feel the same way. They never knock when they come see to us. We would be insulted if they did. Delores loves Marvin nearly as much as she does me, and I loved both Gloria and Patti that way. We've known the twins since they were knee high to a grasshopper, and we feel like their uncles. We know they love us. Just watch when you see them greet us. They hug us with their eyes closed. Did you every have someone in your family you were very close to?"

Eric nodded, and said, "I had a brother. He was killed fighting the French. I think of him every day."

"Well, that's the way Marvin and Charlie are to us. Now, do you understand?"

"Some. My English breeding is hard to overcome, Tim."

Tim said, "I want you to feel about us as we feel about Marvin and Charlie. I understand it will take some time, but we'll get there." Tim then stood and patted Eric on the shoulder.

Eric said, "Thank you, Tim. You are an understanding chap. I can see why you are so well liked."

Tim said, "Charlie told us a long time ago, not to knock as he felt that we owned part of this mansion, because of the work we did."

However, at parties, Eric met the guests at the door with one of his Mexican footmen, who was one of the sons of one of the cowboys that came up from Mexico. Eric tried to train them, and to an extent was somewhat successful.

Eric could tell the boys adored him and tried their best. However, the maids made eyes at him, and were obvious doing it. One of them even put her arm around him and hugged him when something nice happened. She then winked at him.

Life was good, and Lydia had her baby, but Lisa was still not pregnant. Of course they named him, Charlie.

The church had finally accepted them. They had changed parsons, and the new parson knew nothing about the past, and accepted them like everyone else.

A year later, Lisa had a daughter. She looked like Patti except for the hair, and everyone said so. Lisa said, "I guess in twenty years she will want you, Charlie."

Charlie said, 'No, she'll want Marvin, because I'm her dad."

***

Marvin took Lydia back to meet the Randalls after four years. Lydia had two boys who were quite active. Lisa was pregnant when they left.

Mildred loved the kids as if they were her grand children. J. W. got both on one horse, that was extremely tame, and took them riding.

Lydia took Mildred aside and told her about their age different, and that she had been in love with Marvin since she was six.

Mildred said, "Just like Patti. I'm so glad he married you. I could tell he was reluctant at first to marry Patti. However, she taught him to love younger women and broke the ice for you."

"We loved Patti, she never tried to be our mother, she just acted like we were her sisters," said Lydia. "To know Patti was to love her. I told her I had loved Marvin since I was six.

She said, 'Well, when I wear him out, I'll give him to you.' We both laughed until we cried. She was such a delight, Mrs. Randall."

"I'm so glad you got to know her. You now understand how J. W. and I miss her so much."

Marvin could tell that the Randalls loved the boys as if they were their own grandkids. He made a mental note to return at least every other year. Now that there were trains to nearly every town, it would be easy to do.

As they were traveling home, Marvin said, "I started out from Marble Falls to go to California. Why don't just you and I go? Lisa can mind the kids. Both our kids look at her as their second mom, just as her kids do you."

On their way home, Lydia said, "You want to stop in Gallup don't you, Marvin. I want to do that, too. I haven't seen my aunt and uncle since mom died. It will be good to see them again."

After they were home for a couple of weeks, Marvin talked to Charlie and Lisa about their California trip. It was arranged, and they left on the train.

They wrote Tate and Thelma, and gave the date and time they would arrive. They were at the station to meet them.

Thelma said disappointedly, "I thought the kids would be with you."

"Marvin said, "No, we're going to some places that it would be hard to tote them along. Lisa and Charlie are as much their parents as we are, so I don't see them missing us."

Tate had aged some, but Thelma looked the same. She hung on to Tate, and it was obvious how much she loved him.

They stayed two days and were driven all around Gallup. Then they were off again.

They enjoyed Los Angeles. It was much larger than they had imagined. They took a ship to San Diego. It was very pretty. They stayed there three days then took a ship to San Francisco. They had a couple of stops along the way that were nice. They enjoyed the ship, and at night would go to the fantail to watch the surf.

In San Francisco they stayed at a marvelous hotel. It had a show five nights a week, and all the shows were grand. They had shows in Santa Fe, but they weren't nearly in the class of the ones in San Francisco.

They had now been gone two weeks and Lydia said, "I want to go home Marvin. The kids are probably driving Eric up the walls by now."

Marvin nodded and then said, "I don't think they will drive Eric up the wall, he has them trained. He still is uncomfortable with them running and hugging him," and they both smiled.

New Mexico was now allowed a representative to congress although still a territory. When they returned, Charlie said, "I have been nominated to run for congress, Marvin. I think I would like that. I haven't seen Washington, DC in years, and it may be good for Lisa and me."

Charlie won in a landslide. A few months later, they were off to Washington DC. They bought a home in Arlington, close to the river, so Charlie would have a short commute.

In Arlington one day, Charlie was getting a haircut. As he was leaving, an old colleague of his, saw him as he came out the door. It was Paul Vaughn.

They clasped hands and Paul said "How's Adele, Charlie?"

Charlie said, "She was shot and killed some six years ago."

Paul said, "I'm sorry to hear that. She told me when she was leaving to reunite with you, that it would be permanent, then."

"Yes. We had our troubles, but she's at rest now."

"Are you remarried?"

"Yes, I now have two children by my new wife, Lisa. We live here in Arlington. Why don't you and Karan drop by some times." He then gave them his address.

"What are you doing here in Arlington, Charlie?"

"I'm representing the territory of New Mexico in congress."

"My, you have come up in the world, we will certainly be over. We won't drop in though, you will need to invite us as Karan wouldn't drop in on anyone. You and I could drop in on anyone, but these women have to go by some sort of protocol."

When Paul came home and told Karan about meeting with Charlie, she said, "I'm glad Adele's not with Charlie anymore. She slept with Calvin for ten years, and he had five children. I'm glad he got religion and finally quit seeing her. That's the only reason she went back to Charlie. Do you suppose Charlie ever knew that?"

"Of course, that's the reason he went to Santa Fe. She was a looker."

"Yes, and she would have probably slept with you too, had I not clung to you every time we were in her presents. I never saw a woman who could charm nearly any man into her web. She had to have men like I have to have chocolates."

Paul said, "I don't think she was that addicted," and they both laughed.

Karen decided to ask them over first. She sent an invitation only to them. After they accepted, she sent invitations to several of their common friends. A couple of Charlie's friends declined, as they thought Charlie may know of their sleeping with Adele, but others came.

Lisa was introduced. She was young and gorgeous. She had the most marvelous wardrobe possible. Her engagement ring was three carats. Her gown was cut marvelously showing just enough of her female extremities.

Paul was the first to speak and said, "My gosh, Charlie, she's prettier than Adele, and that is going some."

Lisa smiled and said, "I had to wait four years to get him to marry me. I loved him the first time I saw him."

"Well, Charlie is quite a catch. All the women were chasing him until Adele came into the picture. Did you know, Adele?"

Lisa's face turned solemn and she said, "Yes." And that is all she said. Charlie was extremely pleased with her, as Lisa was outspoken, and could have said some terrible things about her, but didn't.

One of the men looked at Charlie and said, "Do you know what happened to Adele?"

"She was killed by a stay bullet while on vacation in Mexico."

The women who knew Adele, thought, *"Stray hell, some wife gunned her down."* Charlie noticed that no one said they were sorry or made any gesture of condolences. He thought, *"They know Adele, and are glad she's dead."*

The party went well and when Paul announced that

Charlie was a United States Congressman, they all clapped and congratulated him.

As they were driving home in their new buggy, Charlie said, "You were magnificent, Lisa."

She said, "I could tell you were on edge when they asked if I knew Adele. Lydia told me before I left, to curb my tongue, as I was now the wife of a U. S. Congressman.

"I could hear her voice yelling at me to shut up, when they asked about Adele. Lydia would be proud of me. I can tell you I would have liked to have talked fifteen minutes telling them what I thought of Adele. To her credit, I will admit Adele had more charm and beauty than anyone I ever met. Some have beauty and some have charm, but few have both."

"You have both," said Charlie.

"You love me so much that you even like my faults, Charlie," and moved over and clutched his arm.

A few months later they were at a ball, Lisa was again the belle of the ball. She had charm, also. She was dancing with another congressman, and Charlie was at the bar getting a drink. An old colleague was there, and was obviously drunk. His name was William Tolliver from Virginia. He saw Charlie and said, "Man, you sure know how to pick 'em. That new wife or yours is as beautiful as Adele. I just hope she doesn't sleep around like Adele."

With that Charlie hit him so hard he knocked the man down and out. Lisa was returning and Charlie took Lisa by the arm, and turned toward the door. He picked up his hat and coat, and they went home."

Charlie was quiet and Lisa knew something very bad had happened. She decided not to ask him. He would tell her if he wanted her to know, but if he didn't tell her, that was okay, too.

Two days hence, two man in formal attire came to his door. They said, "Sir, you have insulted Congressman Tolliver, and he is challenging you to a duel. You can select the weapons and the place. He will be waiting to hear from you. They handed him an envelope that gave an address and left.

Lisa was in the kitchen and said, "Who was that at the door?"

"Just something about next week's business. Do you mind if I go to see Paul Vaughn about that business?"

"No, go ahead. I have somethings I have to do, anyway."

Charlie explained the whole thing to Paul. Paul sat there awhile not saying anything. He then said, "Are you thinking about dueling him?"

"I don't know. I came here for advice."

"Well, on one hand it was his fault. You could say that you won't duel a disreputable rogue like he is. However, many people may think you a coward. Are you skilled with any weapon?"

"No, I've only fired a rifle a couple of times and never a handgun. I know nothing about swords, as I was a paper shuffler during the war. I do think I could beat him with bare fists, but I don't know if that would be acceptable."

"No, I'm afraid not. It must be a gentleman's weapon, and the only two I know are pistols or swords. You could put it off for two weeks, and use that time to practice with a pistol. I have no idea what skills Tolliver has with weapons. I could ask around. You don't have to answer that challenge for a couple of days. That will give us time to find out."

Paul asked around and found that Tolliver was a captain in the cavalry during the war. That meant he was probably skilled with both pistol and sword."

Charlie said, "I shall answer the challenge and tell them pistols. I shall name a date two weeks away and practice everyday. I will need a teacher."

The challenge was answered and Charlie bought a set of dueling pistols. He found a skilled marksman and worked everyday with him. At the end of two weeks, Charlie felt he had an even chance. His instructor and Paul were his seconds. The instructor's last words were, remember, accuracy is more important than all the things I taught you. Make sure you take careful aim no matter if you are hit."

At the time and date, Charlie was there and was terribly nervous. His instuctor said, "Just go through your checklist, and don't think of the duel. Just consentrate on the steps I told you, 'turn sideways, take careful aim and shoot. Aim at the center of his torso."

They walked off the steps and Charlie did his best to consentrate on the checklist. He turned to fire, but his opponent jumped the gun, and shot Charlie as he made his turn. Both seconds fired at Tolliver and killed him. However, Charlie was hit badly in the upper chest. They rushed him to a doctor they had established at a house nearby. The doctor had his nurse and all the equipment he need. That was Paul's idea, and it paid off.

The doctor operated on Charlie immediately, and extracted the lead. He was good at this, as he had taken out many a bullet during the war. He closed up Charlie and said, "I've done all I can. He's is in God's hand's now."

Charlie died an hour later. He knew he was dying and called to Paul. He said, "Tell Lisa that I loved her beyond anyone who has ever lived. She made me the happiest. Write my partner and tell him my last words were how much I loved him."

Charlie then closed his eyes and died."

"Lisa was hysterical when she learned the news. No one could calm her. She got a lady to tend the kids, and drove off in their buggy. She was gone before anyone knew where she was going.

She was gone three days. Finally at dusk, the third day, she arrived. Paul and Karen had not left her house. Both children ran to her crying, and she picked up both, and hugged them. She looked at Paul and said, "I'm alright now. I want to go to Santa Fe. Have you written Marvin?"

"No, we haven't contacted anyone. We had Charlie embalmed, as we knew he would want to be buried in Santa Fe."

She left the next day with the children and the coffin. No one had been notified. She arrive at noon and sent a messenger to get Marvin and Lydia. The message said she was at the depot, and needed a ride. She added, bring a wagon as I have a lot to carry.

As Marvin was putting the traces on the mules, a strange feeling came over him. He said aloud, "The message said, 'I'm at the station,' not we're at the station." He called to Lydia who had said, "I'll wait for them here, as the wagon may be full."

Marvin said, "Come with me Lydia, you may be needed."

When they were near the station Lydia could see Lisa

standing by the coffin that was on a flat tram. The children looked sad. Lisa immediately went into tears. She jumped off the wagon before it came to a stop. She rushed to Lisa and they embrassed. Nothing was said, not even on the way home.

Charlie was put in the dining room. Eric arranged it so that it was in a prominent place. Lydia's children asked, "Who is that?"

Their girl, said, "It's my daddy, and then ran over and hugged the casket. They all cried then, Marvin the most. He even leaned over the casket and hugged it. This just killed Lydia and Lisa as they knew how much Marvin loved Charlie."

They had a memorial at the largest auditorium in Santa Fe, and that was too small. Nearly everyone in Santa Fe came. Many men openly cried.

The crew stood together behind the casket, all in a row. No one else was in that row and Marvin came and joined them. No tears showed, they had their hats were over their hearts and you could tell by their faces it was the hardest time in their lives.

Marvin then spoke. He said:

"Charlie was like a brother to many of us. He was the dearest friend I had. The boys think the same way. He treated each of his boys like they were his brother." He then turned to Lisa and said, "This woman gave him the greatest love any woman could give a man. He told me many times that God had touched him in so many ways. Many in this auditorium were touched by Charlie. Many of us owe our livelihood to Charlie."

Marvin then touched the casket and said, "I love you partner." When he did this, a tear rolled down Tim's face.

It was a few day before anyone said much. After a month Lydia came to Lisa and said, "We will just do what we've always done. When you need Marvin, we'll just swap places. He never knew before, and he won't now."

Lisa said, "You are the sweetest sister in the world. No woman I know loves their sister so much. I do love him as much as Charlie. Should we tell him?"

"No, Lisa, I don't think he's ready yet. He doesn't realize that all the children are his. It's good that we figured out the first year that Charlie was sterile." She laughed then and said, "He can barely keep up as it is. We may put him with Charlie too soon."

"I want you to have his love, Lisa. Remember before we met Charlie, how we both agreed to share Marvin?"

Lisa smiled and said, "Yes, and we never changed our minds. I thank you for sharing him with me through the years."

"I think we should tell him, but I say wait a few weeks and let him get settled and used to Charlie being gone."

Six weeks later, when Lydia was in bed with Marvin she said, "Do you remember when Lisa and I told you we were going to marry you?"

"Yeah, you were about seven, I believe. I thought it was so cute."

"I have a story to tell you, and I'll ask you not to comment until I'm through."

Marvin was puzzled, but he said, "Okay, go ahead."

"The first year we were married we figured out that

Charlie was sterile. So, we made a plan. I would sleep with Charlie and Lisa would sleep with you when her fertile period came around. That's the only way she could have children.

"We made the swap when you and Charlie were in bed and there wasn't much light. After having sex with you both, we would describe in detail how you made love and what you liked. We went over this thoroughly, as we knew there could be no slipups.

"We did certain things that the other would then do, when we were with you and Charlie. That way you would never suspect. We even practiced kissing, so we would do it exactly the same. So, you see we are both married to you Marvin. We will never tell the children, but Lisa is as much your wife as me. What do you say, Marvin?"

"I'm stunned. I remember a couple of times I thought that you seemed like Lisa, but then you would do something that I knew she would not know. You pulled it off, and I now see I'm married to Lisa, too. Where do we go from here?"

"We'll just share you, one at a time of course."

Marvin laughed and said, "Two at a time would never work as I'm not Hercules."

"It will just be our secret. I don't love you any less, and Lisa loves you as much as I do. After all, you're the father of her children."

Marvin said, "I wonder what God thinks of this arrangement?"

"Lisa and I have searched the scriptures and can find no place where having two wives is against God's law. Adultery is, but this is not adultery. We both hold to you as our husband."

"I don't think I will sleep much tonight."

"Why don't I go get Lisa, and the three of us talk awhile?"

Marvin nodded and she left. Lisa appeared and said, "Oh, Marvin, I am so relieved you took this the way you did. I've loved you since I was six. Lydia and I are okay with a plural marriage. We will love you forever."

Lydia said, "Why don't you two sleep together tonight for the first time when Marvin knows it's you." She then left.

Lisa said, "It's like a honeymoon. I'm as giddy as a teenage bride."

Marvin took her in his arms and they came together like they were on a honeymoon.

CHAPTER 19

The Plural Marriage

MARVIN WENT TO Gerald Rollins office. Gerald looked up and said, "To what do I owe the pleasure, Marvin?"

Marvin sat down and said, "I need you to help run all our businesses, now that Charlie's gone. I can assure you the compensation will be better than you make here."

Gerald said, "I think I can handle the land business from Charlie's office. I will have to hire a land man to do the leg work, but I think it will be good for both of us. It will take me awhile to learn everything Charlie did, he was one smart feller."

Gerald did work out. He was innovative, and saw many thing that could be improved or started. Marvin was more than pleased with his creativity.

One day Gerald snapped his fingers and said, "You know Charlie's wife could handle the leg work of the land business. She probably needs to keep busy, now that Charlie's gone. Why don't you tell her we need her now. We don't even have to pay her."

"My gosh, Gerald, you are a sly fellow. That is shear genius. I'll go get her right now, so we can both talk to her."

In a half hour Lisa was there and said, "Why do you want to talk to me, Gerald?"

Marvin started by saying, "Lisa, now that Charlie's gone, he left a pretty large hole in the business. I needed Gerald in Charlie's chair. He still has his land business to run, and he won't have time to show people the properties. Then he came up with the solution. It was pure genius. He thought of you. You need to know the workings of this business anyway, and for that matter, Lydia, does too. However, one of you needs to be with the children. I know Mrs. Knowlton does a fine job with them, but they need the presents of their mom. You both are moms to all the children.

"What do you say about coming to work with us. You will have an office here. I plan on moving all of Gerald's business here. That will take constructing an addition to this building, but it needs renovating anyway. We have to expand our offices with you coming, and you can give us some ideas in that department."

"I never thought of working here, but it's a marvelous idea, Gerald. You **are** a genius. I am thrilled that you thought of me. I'll start tomorrow."

Gerald said, "I'll have to work with you everyday as there is a lot to learn. Most of the training is land laws. I will give you a handbook, and you and Lydia can go over it until it's practically memorized.

Lisa couldn't wait to tell Lydia. Marvin and she left for their house. Lydia was thrilled, too. Marvin said, "As soon as some of the children are in school, we plan on bringing you into the office, also, Lydia. You both know you will have to run this business someday."

"Don't even talk like that, if both of you leave us, we will have to marry Eric." Eric was standing there and said, "I beg your pardon," and they all laughed.

After the first year, Lisa was great at her job. She sold properties like hot cakes.

Gerald said, "Damn, I had no idea she would be that good at this or I would have had her working with me the day I came to work. Her beauty mesmerized her clients. Then her glib tongue closes the deal. I bet when Lydia comes to work, we'll drive the other land offices out of business."

Lydia came to work in the fall when the kids returned to school, and both girls were marvelous. They also learned about all the other businesses.

One thing they didn't think of was Lisa becoming pregnant, which she did.

Lisa said, "We'll just do what mama did when she was pregnant with us. She left town, but before going, told the town people she was going away to help her cousin have a baby."

When Lisa was five months pregnant she went to Albuquerque and then on to Gallup. She stayed with Thelma and Tate and had the baby there. It happen, both Lisa and Lydia became pregnant at the same time. When Lydia reached her eight month she left for Gallup. She told everyone that she needed her aunt Thelma. The babies were born, and they told everyone that Lydia had twins.

When the girls returned, Marvin never knew which one was in his bed. They kissed and made love identically. He loved them both and told Lisa that. They now had eight children. The last were two little girls born on the same day. Everyone in their family believed them twins. They looked just like twins.

Marvin said, "I never imagined we could fill Cordova's house, but we nearly have.

Mrs. Bowers was talking to the new parson and said, "I do believe that brother Ellis has two wives. I bet he can't tell them apart. They both hold onto him during the service like newly weds. My gosh they've been married twelve years, you'd think that they would have cooled off by now."

"Some people never cool off. I knew this couple........I had better not tell that story."

"Oh please Reverend, you have piqued my curiosity to where I have to know."

"You must never tell anyone this story, and especially that you heard it from me."

He told the story, and Mrs. Bowers was fanning herself by the end.

Her husband was surprised that night. He thought she was twenty years younger, as she was all over him. She was forty-two years old, and became pregnant. The rumor's were now flowing again.

No one ever knew that Marvin was married to both the twins. They were all in love and lived out their lives that way. The two girls, who were born the same day, turned out to look just like their mothers. Lisa and Lydia were observing them on Marvin's lap hugging and kissing him. Lydia said, "They may take Marvin away from us in twelve to fifteen years," and both of them laughed. Lisa said, we best keep an eye on them.

The End

Printed in the United States
By Bookmasters